Adam & Adeline

For My Dearest Mother
Thanks for enduring

- & -

For Anna
*But for your courage and forthrightness to speak
the truth and take a stand in the name of Christ,
these pages would yet be marred and the story
lingering still in darkness.*

Chapters

Chapter 1: Magic...7

Chapter 2: Reality...17

Chapter 3: Chemistry.......................................29

Chapter 4: Fury...69

Chapter 5: Chemistry.......................................79

Chapter 6: Reality.. 147

Chapter 7: Love.. 153

Closing Letter: From Wayward Paths.................... 171

Chapter 1
Magic

dam was his name. Hers was Adeline. And they met, as most often do: upon the convergence of two worlds—specifically, when she'd arrived at Enderbrine's School of Enchantment for her first semester, and there met a young lad, also newly enrolled, sitting near the back in her third period class, Transmutational Tutelage and Training.

Theirs was a story of which most can wish only to boast, for never before had such passionate attraction been born out of mere sight. Neither would have ever admitted to believing in such rapture upon first glance, for truly neither ever had. But, when finally the moment came for their eyes to meet, it was made sure in both minds that some things in life really can be that simple.

And so it was: a simple romance—but this, I'm afraid to say, is not wholly a tale of that particular time, nor is it one in which a happy ending can be found.

It may be a bit off-putting for a reader to hear the manner in which a story concludes, with no more than a handful of paragraphs invested. And yet, here I am declaring rather plainly that this tale has not what many would call an uplifting finale.

Or, does it?

I suppose it will depend on the position from which you choose to observe. For me, your omniscient storyteller within the lines, I see both sides equally, and thusly tell the tale. Therefore, I say the ending arrives most monotonously, because I take no particular side. If one character ends his or her journey on a happy note, and the other on one born from a poorly tuned and recently-run-over-by-a-bulldozer piano, I must, in good conscience, inform you that the tale you are about to read meets not all the requirements for bliss. Think of it this way: If white were a happy ending, and black were tragic, and the two were mixed together, the result is not wholly happy or wholly tragic. In grey, it is up to you to see either the white or the black.

How stands the water level in *your* glass, dear reader?

Now, one might argue that happy endings always (or, usually) require regrettable ends for a villain or an antagonist. Though a less than desirable end (desirable as defined by the standards of the villain) befalls one of the main characters, we can still rejoice in the triumph of the heroes—can we not? But have we a clear-cut hero and villain (or, *villains*) in this tale? I'll leave that to you. For me, as I'd mentioned earlier, both shall be seen as equals, as a pair of sweethearts on a collision course with themselves, equally sound and flawed, admirable and despicable in their own respects. And, therefore, in order for a happy ending to be declared, a mutual, merry outcome would be required—and, I regret to say, there is none.

Perhaps this is just the way of life—of course it is! Life is neither wholly happy nor wholly tragic. And, for you, dear reader, it would seem that, in choosing this narrative to satisfy your need for diversion, a mad-dashing escape has been made from the cacophony of Life and right into the waiting arms of Life.

You can thank the Author for that.

I'm just the narrator.

***

Our tale begins deep in the mountains—which range specifically,

I cannot say; for such a divulgence of information would only compromise the privacy of him who presently lives there, and leave his mailbox stuffed to the bursting point with fan letters, the sheer volume of which he is scarce likely to read in his lifetime. Besides, the focal character about whom I am to speak doesn't even live there anymore! No; a man named Leroy now calls that patch of land home, having one day stumbled upon the deserted and decaying remnants of—oh, well; that's another story.

Anyway, as I was saying before my digression, our tale begins in the mountains, in a dark and dreary mansion, molded from the very peak on which it stands. A handsome place, this mansion, built specifically to the liking of its master, who, if you will believe my saying so, built the place entirely by himself. Of course, such a statement is, on its face, rather believable; however, if I may elaborate on the layers within, we shall test your capacity for faith in the realm of wonder.

When I say the master had built the place singlehandedly, not only do I mean it was of his specific design, but also that he personally placed every brick, painted every wall, affixed every fixture, arranged every piece of furniture, sculpted every ornament, and chiseled every rock from the body of the mighty mountain itself. Furthermore, if your mind has not already broken beneath the weight of this phenomenon, the master placed every brick, painted every wall, affixed every fixture, arranged every piece of furniture, sculpted every ornament, and chiseled every rock from the body of the mighty mountain itself...all in a single day.

But from sun to sun he did not toil—no, indeed! He managed to erect, furnish, sculpt, and decorate the entire mountainous manner in a matter of minutes—*one* minute to be…well, misleading, actually. One *moment* would be a more accurate way to put it.

And, finally, if what I have said thus far has not already left you baffled, let me tell you that he accomplished this feat with a mere flick of the wrist!

Pray tell, O faithful fabulist, how can it be so? I can hear you say. *For surely such miracles belong not to the race of man!*

Indeed, you are correct, my dear, eloquent reader.

Such miracles are, unfortunately, impossible for the likes of man.

"But, c'mon, how super cool would it have been if I *had* done that? All with just a flick of the wrist! One flick, and *POOF!* Or, do you think it would be more of a *BANG* sound? Maybe a *POP?*"

"I think 'POP' is *exactly* how it sounded," said Adeline with a giant roll of the eyes.

"*Har har,*" returned a sarcastic laugh from the partially smiling lips of Adam, who had been pacing about before her, acting out the instantaneous construction of the lavish structure in which they lounged, and had only now turned his eyes to meet the intended recipient of his discourse, breaking them away from their most beloved of places: the wall-sized mirror, in which he had very much enjoyed watching his handsome face and frame tell the tale of his fantastical greatness, with grand gestures, striking poses, smoldering smolders, and tons of tousles through his near-shoulder-length, timber-colored hair.

"Exactly!" Adeline declared, sitting bolt upright and tossing back onto the silver platter beside her the vine of grapes she'd been enjoying. "Just like *that!* 'POP! P*aaaaaaahh*p!'" she shouted, doing a whiny soprano version of Adam's voice, and flicking her wrist in the air. "*Pop*, I don't *wanna* build my own house—it's too *har-har-haaaaaaard*."

"Oh, and these dainty piggies—" chuckled Adam, rushing to Adeline and playfully grabbing her fingers, "—you're telling me that *these* guys cut even one plank of the wood, or drove even one of the nails holding them together, over at *your* place?"

"Of course not!" she giggled, as Adam nuzzled in beside her on the chesterfield. "I have a *POP*, too, you know."

And, before even you, dear reader, could slam shut the covers of this book and rush to the toilet to give a pre-hurl dry heave before the cliché, over-done, mushy stupid stuff found in every book of campy romance ever written leaps off the page and infects your gut with a nauseating mawkishness and your throat with a most potent gag, the pair had commenced a spirited shoving match. Tittering like the school children they were, it had started with an exchange of soft shoves, but had hastily morphed into a competitive dealing of increasingly smart blows, the final of which, delivered from Adeline with the full of her weight behind her, upended Adam from the chesterfield and sent him rolling speedily toward the tiny table on which sat the goldfish bowl containing the goldfish that hadn't been fed since the summer fair in which it had been won, floating inside and upside-down, indifferent to the swiftly approaching product of teenage folly. One smart bump against the neck, and the table weeble-wobbled and sent the goldfish bowl and its yellowed water sailing through the autumn air on a posthumous (or, in this case, would it be post-*piscis*?) revenge trajectory: colliding with Adam's skull, resulting in a *CLUNK* and shatter so satisfying, we can but wonder if the poor, deceased marinefellow didn't give a delighted smirk from beyond the grave.

When at last Adam's eyes had rolled out from within his head, where they had been absentmindedly admiring the vast atrium of empty space within his cranial dome, they beheld and relayed to his concussed coconut the image of Adeline, kneeling beside him and crying with laughter, while a damp rag patted his cheeks, and stinging rushes of frost seeped through his forehead.

"It was in your nose!" she squealed mirthfully. "What are the *odds?*"

Adam could make neither head nor tail of this, until a shriveled, eyeless goldfish carcass was held up by the tail to his face, its gaping mouth and hollow head gazing dumbly back at his own.

"Did you ever name it?" said Adeline, sniffling and wiping her eyes; a rogue chuckle and a pair of its snickering buddies managed also to escape her diaphragm as she did so.

Adam's bug-eyed stare worked tirelessly to put together the pieces of the focal object, while his mind raced for a name by which to identify it.

"Bubble," he mumbled at length.

"You idiot!" cried Adeline with a hearty guffaw and a playful shove to the arm that felt more like a lightning bolt striking the body. "What a dumb name! Bubble, Bubble!" she said, donning her best Shakespearian voice and lifting Bubble's corpse high into the air, as might one the skull of Yorick. "You're in trouble! Left to grumble, bod to crumble; and now you lie amongst the rubble!"

Better than Hamlet's version of that "double-bubble-trouble" speech, thought she, tossing her long, sunny locks over her shoulders and filling her chest with a gust of pride taken in through her nostrils. (Enderbrine's wasn't exactly known for its courses on the works of Shakespeare, else she might have known better).

"Okay, okay!" grunted Adam, squeezing shut his eyes and giving Adeline a not-too-gentle shove. "Knock it off—my head is pounding."

"Flat in puddle, head befuddled, like fire burns—let's make it *double*!"

With that, Adeline lifted a hand to strike; but Adam's eyes snapped the world back into focus and caught her arm mid-swing before it could meet its mark.

It had been a playful swing, one delivered, in fact, with no intent to make impact, but rather as bait so that the true strike could meet its target without resistance.

"Oooh," Adeline purred, her right hand still held high in his grasp. "Wits endure when world is muddled."

As those soft syllables washed over Adam's twitching face like the warm, summer sweat of a honey comb, a tiny hand slithered undetected over his right shoulder to his unguarded and exposed right cheek; and there, with a fingertip tap, like the *tink* from a tinker's tiny hammer, she delivered a smart yet gentle blow.

However, for the receiving end of the impish smite, she might as well have had flaming anvils for fingertips.

"*AH!*" cried Adam, as his brain jostled about in his head. "WHAT TH—"

But before any further frustrated fire could scorch the air, the flames were swallowed hole and his lips were sealed by those of another.

Moments like these, if taking only the accounts of those experiencing them, are often difficult to gauge in regard to duration; but, for the party of the first part, it seemed as if it were the perfect amount of time; and, for the party of the second part, it seemed not nearly long enough.

One fire had been quelled; another was born.

Adam absorbed every visible element of every moment; Adeline, eyes sealed, let the scene meld with her very being; until the fire that had both quelled and ignited was separated, the flame left behind seeking now what sort of fuel was to be found in the patch of earth in which it had been released.

Eventually, the pair sat gazing at one another, the oceans in their eyes churning with increasing intensity. Adam could see clearly in Adeline's a great and mighty wave, lost somewhere deep within both; lost, knowing no genesis, nor terminus, nor direction; a wild wave, crashing violently against the face of a grand, towering rock, rising out of the sea.

Then, suddenly, a deep crimson filled Adeline's face, and her mouth became like a barren desert.

Sealing her lips, she swallowed hard and, trembling, retreated quickly.

Though still feeling as if his head were attached to the hose of an air compressor, Adam lifted his body onto one elbow and eyed Adeline with some concern.

Before he could conjure something to say, however, Adeline leapt to her feet and said through a jaw intent on quivering against her will, "I have to go."

"But—"

"I'll see you in class tomorrow," she said, backing slowly to the door. "It was nice to meet you."

With that, she disappeared into the hall.

Adam sat dumbly on the floor awhile, counting the clicks of her heels as she descended the marble staircase in the grand foyer; two hundred and twenty-seven clicks he counted before the sound could no longer reach his ears.

It had been one of those days, the kind that are so familiar, and yet never actually happen.

Adeline: Perhaps the only Magic to be found at Enderbrine's.

Chapter 2
Reality

*O*ne needs neither affluence nor influence to get into Enderbrine's. Anyone can enroll. However, if one is the son or daughter of an Enderbrinian alumnus, one is automatically predisposed—er, that is—pre*qualified* for admittance.

While it is true that not every child of an Enderbriner finds within the walls of the well-known School of Enchantment a seat with his or her name printed upon it, generational influence has ever been a tremendous indicator of one's intrinsic remarkability (or, at least, one's thorough indoctrination thereof), as well as one's unique educational path. But such students are expected; the mold-breakers are the ones Enderbrine's truly loves best: the first generation Magic-weavers that will surely produce and inspire a new age of posteriors to fill the institution's ever-populating seats, growing rooms, and expanding halls.

First impressions of Enderbrine's are most often formed off-campus, some by way of the testimonies mumbled from the lips of those who had once trod about its halls, recalling well that which existed about and below ankle-level, and vaguely (if at all) everything else; other impressions are formed from pure supposition. One's second impression, therefore, is usually quite underwhelming: the actual beholding the school itself. If one's eyes could be bothered to gaze forward for more than three seconds, one might note a big building, some grass, stone walkways, and—oh, what*ever*, am I right? Eyes down again, per usual.

Indeed, what I have just relayed is about as much as any student could relay to you, should you be so fortunate as to receive a reply to any query posed to someone who would pass right through you as through a ghost—and even *this* might be more than you could expect to hear! Still, there is a persistent patch of mud near the entrance, which, being that it is located in the optical range of the typical student, is known to practically everyone; of its stubborn perseverance, there exist a host of theories. Few, however, actually know its purpose; and not one among this diminutive group can be called a student.

Enderbrine's is a typical social place: kids see everybody, but behold no one. Names and faces are the currency shuttled and shuffled along the endless webs weaved between classrooms; and status is determined, as often it is, by one's stockpile of the dominant currency's definition: its gold standard, if you will.

A place of learning is Enderbrine's; though, perhaps not in the same way as you, dear reader, might have assumed when your eyes beheld the word "school" attached to its name. Already we know the institution gained not its fame from its excellent courses and insightful lectures on the works of Shakespeare, and one would be hard-pressed to find any course aligned with what its instructors would call "convention"—factual theories and theoretical facts is probably the best way to describe the two arms of education whence all courses branch. And welcomed with opened arms to the churning machine are the young and the colorful, who, having emerged with hues dulling from their first two phases of education, enter here into the final, third phase (which looks a great deal like the first two), where they might shed that color completely and don the standard hue that fills the minds and spirits of all successful pieces of work: a color dubbed "unique," painted and worn with visceral pride upon all whose minds are made different by instruction in an accepted standard of thought, whose quickly atrophying hands

have been fitted with correcting braces that they might properly forge beauty, and whose collective indistinguishability breeds
acceptance and reassurance in the spotlighted path along which
graduates are corralled: a path upon which not a single beam of
that light does show, as each blinding lamp is directed intently at
the gaping eyes from the hollowed heads set above them, while
below the marching feet keep pace to the drum of independent
conformity, storming straight and true, relentlessly, passing in
uniform lines into the all-consuming night.

You might well picture Enderbrine's as a sort of university
or a specialized institution of higher education; although, with
students whose genesis and exodus occur in the teenage years
(and, sometimes, in reverse order—a most extraordinary Magic,
indeed), even I cannot tell if Enderbrine's equates best to what
we would call a college or to a high school. Enderbrine's is many
things, including a mystery none can spare a moment to solve.

But, above all else, Enderbrine's is a place of Magic, where
one is affirmed that anything is possible if they will only believe,
and if others can be convinced to provide it. Magic lies inside
each and every unique and beautiful snowflake who attends, and
it is up to each individual flake to discover and identify it—and
sometimes create it, if need be. Day by day, instructors query
for direction their masters, seated row on row before them; they
meet outstretched hands and lifted eyes, not with touch and
recognition, but rather with an example of palms buried within
the chest and eyes cast downward, until the classroom walks
about with arms lodged nearly elbow-deep inside chest cavities
and eyes firmly fixed upon the floor, leading to much butting of
bodies and heads—this, indeed, is an Enderbrinian instructor's
greatest offering: to bestow said sovereigns with the Magic to

further and elevate his or her own understanding by drawing directly from said understanding and whatever else had by fumbling fingers been found within the instructor's own isolated cardiac chamber.

Each student is, in this manner, formed into something soft and edible, prepared to a certain tongue's perfection by hands of molding heated just below the boiling point.

A great, wide world exists beyond the walls of Enderbrine's, and all of it fits within the palm of a student's hand. Microscopic in relative measures, that world can be generally comprehended in its totality, its vast complexities made simple; and via Magic can it be changed to the beholder's liking: one need only speak the Magic Words—though, often mere speech fails to exact the desired change; thus, screaming is the music of the Enderbrinian halls. It is effective Magic; though, much of what is conjured for the purpose of altering seems only to affect the reality of the spell-caster, resulting in many a cannibalistic quarrel whenever two spells collide—this has developed into an increasing issue, as incantations have become a great deal more complex and convoluted over time, to the point of contradiction and confusion regarding stated ends that, at their core, have always spawned from the same shoddy seed. And whenever hexes born of this Magic and cast forth into the microscopic realm are revealed inefficacious, one either withdraws from Enderbrine's, or is sent to the school nurse to have fingers removed from eyes and metal rods extricated from ears. A great many blind and deaf enchanters and enchantresses wander those halls.

That's Enderbrine's.

And already I have dished out more truth than its entire curriculum.

***

Third period, Transmutational Tutelage and Training, was next on this sunniest of sunny days. Not only was this the last day of the school week, which meant abbreviated class periods and an early official release, but it was also and moreover the day Adeline awoke with a striking revelation that would change her life forever: she was in love.

Now, she would argue that she knew it was love right away—of course she would have! It was love—she'd seen it, there, in his eyes; she'd sensed it in her own ocular orbs; it was in the beating of her heart the day they met, in the overwhelming exhilaration that had churned through her veins the first time her hand fell into his; love was unmistakably the way his voice had played like heavenly music to her heart, how his kiss had made her fly; love was the preoccupation of thought and the anticipation of a repeat performance of all these wonderful things. Love was something she'd known would one day come: her first and only, the very thing for which she had waited and had other prospective hands scorned. It was something that had made her behave as never before: so out of character, so free, so liberated, so wild and wonderful! Oh, how long had she known the entrapping walls of her shell—'twas love had broken through and brought forth an Adeline made anew! Love was something that hadn't since gone stale, that hadn't flatlined—or, at least, hadn't been allowed to do so. Love was that *feeling*: the feeling assuring her that what she was feeling was in fact love, *true* love, and not just emotion.

Yes, the truest of true love it was! It was here, and here to stay—thus spoke the revelation of the morn; and on the wings

of that revelation she floated into third period, regretful that it would be an abbreviated one with less time to absorb him, as she had the day they'd met, but grateful that the rest of the day would be theirs to share. How she longed to capture him in a moment of past and present: sitting there in the desk beside hers, his attention fixed upon her every movement, and his heart beating to the pace of her breathing. It had been a most exciting school year; and with the summer holiday waiting just a week around the corner, the expectations for drinking in even more of this wonderful sensation of true love made her like a helium-filled bubble: cast gaily about in the wind, and primed to shoot straight to the moon, or explode into a zillion, multicolored raindrops. And so sailed this bubble from the abbreviated but arduously eternal melded mess that was first period (Structured Spell-Casting and Sorcerous Speech Synchronization) and second period (Yore a Problem: Making History Magical), and into the ever-blessed third period, there to lay her adoring eyes upon her overflowing well of love and his beaming, beautiful face looking right smack dab into the hideous mug of oh-my-GOSH-that's-SHELLY-hanging-ALL-OVER-him-and-he's-SMILING-and-his-ARM-is-wrapped-around-HER—WHAT-THE-*HECK*-IS-*HAPPENING*??

"ADAM!" shrieked Adeline as she burst into a zillion dark and stormy raindrops and descended like a screeching bolt of lightning from the booming bosom of a black cloud. "WHAT ARE YOU—"

"Indoor tones, miss Adeline," came the soft and feathery voice of her instructor. "Remember, our tones are a source of great Magic that can either harm or—"

But before a refresher course could be relayed on the sanctity of fellow eardrums, Adam was on his back in a pile of splintered wood and metal bars, with Adeline beating on his chest with her tiny fists, while Shelly, though momentarily stunned by the force of Adeline's swan dive into Adam's ribs, fumbled about in her backpack for a book large enough to deliver some damage—Enderbrine's books being so small, this was a bit of a dig; but she eventually clasped her dainty paws upon the titanic text *Witch and Warlock: Affronting Words and Wounding Acts, Unabridged Version.*

The next thing Adeline knew, she was sitting in an armchair with a throbbing head and a red-hot ear, while a frigid bead of sweat ran a sluggish path down her forehead, calling forth goosebumps from their mysterious hiding places.

Adam sat across from her.

His lip was swollen and cut along the edge; his hair was a mess, and his clothes were slightly torn. But his flesh and attire did not look half so ugly as the mien painted as if with gravel and tar across his face.

"What the heck, Ad?" he grumbled when at last her fluttering eyes opened and focused upon him.

She had been so high up in the clouds, floating like a bubble, ready to again sup the sweetness of true love and be given wings on which to soar ever higher, only to have had those wings clipped midflight and be sent nose-diving toward a most violent and heartbreaking crash, that all of reality since her waking had felt like a dream. Perhaps she had not yet left that dream whence she'd believed to have awoken; perhaps this was her unconscious mind exploring her greatest bliss and deepest fears, letting her feel both love and heartbreak, and bringing her to a perfervid belief in both.

But the more she looked at him, the more she knew this was indeed the here and now, the real deal, the vivid world of the waking; and in it there was naught but mind-scorching confusion.

Adeline searched for something to say, but for a while she could find nothing.

Adam's sour glare only intensified as the silence persisted.

"Who knew you were one of the *crazy* ones?" he hissed. "Gosh, it's like—*ugh*! You never can tell, can you?"

Adeline could but stare dumbly across the room at Adam.

"Seriously!" he continued through gritted teeth, "What's your deal? Why all of a sudden with this *psycho*-girl stuff?"

Her jaw quivering violently, Adeline barely managed to release a single syllable.

"Why?"

"*Why*? Why, WHAT? *Shelly*? Don't tell me this is about Shelly?"

A tear formed along the rim of Adeline's eye, threatening to fall.

"Oh my *gosh*! *Seriously*? You're gonna flip on me because of *Shelly*?"

"Adam…"

"What ever happened to the old-fashioned types, huh? The ones that could be contented with what they've got—where are *those* girls?"

"But…I thought we…"

"Oh, no! Don't you start with *that*! *We*? Since when are we a *WE*?"

Adeline could find no words—there would have been not an ounce of strength to lift them, anyway.

That tear doubled in size and trembled as it gazed over her eyelid at the rosy hill below.

"You've got *your* list, just like I've got mine! So, what's the big deal?"

"List?" came Adeline's voice at length, softly, weakly.

"Don't play dumb! Everyone's got a list! You've got one, and so do I! And you and I are no different to each other than any one of the names on *either* of them!"

Her head was spinning. This was all too much too fast, and out of such a far left field that she knew not what point to address first.

Rather involuntarily, she muttered between silent bursts of sharp, rattling inhales, "D-do...do you...?"

"What?" barked Adam, straining against his interest to hear her.

"Do...do you love her, Adam?" she asked, eyes red behind a wall of tears, gazing at the floor. "Shelly...do you love her?"

Adam's nostrils flared; smoke from pulverizing teeth leaked through the gaps in his snarling lips.

"No," he growled. "I don't love Shelly...or Charlotte, or Ursula, or Morgan, or Melanie—or *YOU*!"

Adam's final spew might as well have been a bullet sailing straight through her chest.

Save for a droning echo in Adeline's ears that seemed not to gain nor lose any power, and the vibrations of the tear teetering on her eyelid, all was silent.

There was nothing more to say—nothing more she *could* say; and nothing more, she hoped, he would say.

Rising slowly, she drifted like a dense fog to the door, her eyes barely able to remain open or see through the rippling walls before them.

Her heart had been beaten into exhaustion and despair; it was all she could do to place her hand upon the doorknob.

Unable to turn it, however, she dropped her head against the door, as every last shred of strength failed and her face began to contort, while through her swelling throat climbed a sob.

But before that sob could be released, or that single tear fall from her eyelid, the door was suddenly swung open. The force of the swing shot through Adeline's arms and chest, throwing her head backward; but so great was the whiplash that her head immediately rebounded and met the still swinging door (pun warning) *head*-on, casting her, upon the strident impact, into pitch darkness.

When she awoke some time later, her forehead throbbing with both fire and ice, Adam was gone; and letting that tear fall at last—figuratively speaking, of course, as the original, hesitant tear had been during the collision jettisoned into oblivion—Adeline razed the floodgates and sobbed.

Chapter 3
Chemistry

If gossip is the wildfire flame ravaging the halls of Enderbrine's, relationship drama is napalm. The dry and hallow trees roaming the halls of the school of enchantment can be swallowed whole by even the tiniest spark; thus, any sort of story about a fellow empty, rotting log—supposedly bearing such signs of rot as have never been seen among the rotting—has the potential to (and does, practically every time) spread, and spread quickly. But even a fire's fuel needs a point of inception; and at Enderbrine's, that point, that spark, that lighted cigarette amongst the dried leaves, that inflamed, gasoline-soaked rag stuck into a bottle of alcohol, that fiery cannonball hurling toward a hill of fully-filled bottles of lighter fluid, that frantically flailing pyromaniac with his hair aflame and sprinting blindly in the direction of the precariously placed Karl's Kerosene Kabin, set in the midst of a forest on a dry and breezy summer's day—yes, that incendiary source of untempered combustion is none other than the Meddlers Observing Scandals, Quarrels, and Unstable Individuals: Teenage Overlords of Enderbrine's Society.

M.O.S.Q.U.I.T.O.E.S. swarm the halls of Enderbrine's, seeking students succulently swollen with spicy secrets, scrumptious sadness, and saucy stories; such serves to supply the salivating suckers with a super-abundance of savory sustenance, sufficient to spur the sin-seekers onto more secretive secrets, sadder sadnesses, and even saucier stories—sometimes sowing said stories themselves, lest a shortage of sauce for the sucking serve to starve the esurient swarm.

It had been a nasty, humid, and terribly buggy summer's month in the final weeks before the winter break, when it had been reported to M.O.S.Q.U.I.T.O.E.S. that Harry Oliver had been caught waxing his back in the locker room. What students had until then assumed to have been merely a shaggy, woolen undershirt that Harry hardly washed, routinely deodorized, meticulously combed, and from which occasionally plucked the small, white flake of dust (which could, like Magic, be seen scurrying about, as if teased by the passing breeze, and even cast a "dusty head" spell upon the curious), turned out to be his own plenteous pelage; and what other creature but a werewolf could appear so human, and yet boast the coat of a wild animal? Thus, Harry (who would return post-winter-break donning the new moniker Nary—Nary Norbert Edward Moore, was his full name) became the recipient of hurling insults and cries of woe, not to mention more flung silver knives and fired silver bullets than Harry's local bank teller could count in a single trip. (Honestly, Harry made out like a bandit during this time; and he lived to shake off the trauma of his school days and not mind it after all; for, presently, he resides wherever the sky is sunny by day and clear by night, wearing garments woven from the whiskers of snow leopards and the nostril hairs of northern hairynosed wombats, sipping crimson wine atop his silver yacht (The Lonny) and stargazing with his pale, svelte, and befanged wife, Stella, resting tenderly under his arm, watching, waiting for that transformative satellite of the night).

But harry Harry Oliver wasn't the only casual casualty of M.O.S.Q.U.I.T.O.E.S.' swarming; a great many others suffered, as well. Kids wearing t-shirts depicting full moons were tackled into classrooms whenever Harry walked by; some were even charged as his followers if said shirts depicted howling wolves. A quiet and reserved group of students—enthusiasts of dark clothing and matching eye makeup—were cast into their most feared arena: the spotlight; and there were they harassed by hysterical classmates, who pressed garlic cloves against their sniffling sniffers and peeled back their lips to examine the canines, hoping to discover among the beleaguered, bedeviled, and just plain petrified lot one who could deliver the school from the roaming threat. But the more the cacophonous chaos grew, the more the beating wings of M.O.S.Q.U.I.T.O.E.S. hummed, elevating over the noise until the tumult had at last encroached within spitting distance, at which time the wings beat harder, bedlam ballooned, and the cycle continued.

The feast that was Harry (now Nary), however, pales in comparison to the overflowing smorgasbord set forth before M.O.S.Q.U.I.T.O.E.S. when news of Adam and Adeline reached their colony. Adam and Adeline had never been the storied relationship, the superstar pair that had dazzled everyone with their romance; but they were the couple that had broken up in one of the most storied manners humanly possible—on what could M.O.S.Q.U.I.T.O.E.S. *not* feed?

Adam suffered some ridicule, as he had been absolutely body-slammed into submission by a girl who M.O.S.Q.U.I.T.O.E.S. had once reported would never leave the house on a windy day without first filling her sneakers with coins and her pockets with marbles, sometimes tying a dumbbell to the belt loop of her jeans if the forecast called for any gusts over twelve miles per hour. But his attitude toward and interactions with his female peers had become well documented—'twas common knowledge...except to Adeline; and this was the focus of M.O.S.Q.U.I.T.O.E.S.' torment.

The youth of Enderbrine's are taught rather early (and many

of them well before setting foot into the school) that of all Magic there is none more cheap and common than Love. This, of course, is not how it is textually or verbally presented—at least, not in explicit terms; but it is precisely how it has ever been demonstrated and exercised. It is the opinion of the Enderbrine's Academic Administration that Love, as known of old, is an incomplete (and, perhaps, slightly flawed) institution. So defining it, the school inspired a (to use their words) "Movement of the Mind" that had through sealed eyes awoken unto new understandings—one of which was that Love was merely Magical Inspiration—an ingredient, if you will, in the spells that form within each Magic Maker. 'Twas, in fact, less of a redefine, and rather more of an *un*define; and it gave new life to an old question, for which there had once been a concrete answer, but which held now a gaping void: What is Love?

For the latter query, the answer became that there was no answer, at least no answer that could be found or comprehended outside of the heart; for there, surely, within the heart, lay that which could be called love: one could feel it, one was compelled by it, one was anxious for it, one craved it, one knew satisfaction lay within it, and one knew that it was all one needed—one simply *knew* that.

This Movement of the Mind quickly realized that love was not complex, nor was it simple: it was easy; and to it one could be led, if one would only follow that which had whispered the answer to the burning questions and countless desires, and had made right and true that which possessed such power and emotion, so as to declare it simply could not be wrong.

And, so, with the heart at the helm, many a youth explored the variety of colors found within this thing called love; and over the years, the newly named "Love Magic" had been stripped of all its old-fashioned rules and definitions. It was no longer something rooted in anything in particular; it was no longer something produced after a great deal of study and careful contemplation of its complex, and yet rather simple, intricacies; but, rather, it was a spell: an easy, self-serving show of sparks and twinkling lights that dazzled the eyes and infected those at whom it was cast with flashes of intoxicating heat and mind-fogging sensations. They were rather exciting spells, but their potency was inconsistent—perhaps diminishing is a better word: bigger and brighter sparks and twinkles would be required every subsequent time, if any effect was to be had.

But, before any sort of compelling Magic could be tried on another, one needed first to perfect a love spell on oneself. Properly done, one could feel confident in his or her love ability—yet, even the most adept self-hexing pupils encountered baffling problems. It was as if certain people just didn't respond to self-perfected love!

It grew into a real mess.

Love spells eventually became so chaotic, theoretical, feral, and indefinable, that rules became wrong, definitions stifling, and foundations oppressive, to the point where this love was so widely and wildly wielded, everyone had known its taste and had seen (though, most chose to ignore) that its nectar bore an empty value. Many, eventually (often quickly), discovered that, between people, love was a laborious thing, giving rise, as a result, to the use of synthetic outlets that targeted the love sensation, offering the same release and keeping pace, for the most part, with the ever-increasing and harder-to-please demand. Thus, love was a cheap spell; and most who sampled its fruits became addicted to the doomed pursuit of creating the best version of it, or remained ever in a vicious cycle of rinse-and-repeat.

And this is precisely where we find Adam: a rinser and re-peater: wielding and receiving until the sparks and twinkles no longer razzled or dazzled, then moving on to the next brand of the same stuff. Such can be likened to one desiring canned fruit: he buys from the same supplier for a while, until eventually switching to a can dressed with a different label, and then becomes with that label infatuated until boredom sets the eyes upon another container of the same stuff, just differently dressed.

This, however, was nothing. Adam was no unique case. Male and female Enderbriners alike behaved in this manner—it was both accepted and expected. Love was recreational, like buying candy: cheap and (though, perhaps, not the healthiest thing) mostly harmless—you might lose a tooth or two, but what the heck? No one bought the silly stories of old, in which Love, as if some person or entity, would win the day, or could be an all-consuming *whatever it was* to some sap or other.

No one bought this children's storybook stuff.

Except Adeline.

This had now been made known to the entire school.

And, boy, did she ever pay for it.

"There she is!" squealed a M.O.S.Q.U.I.T.O.E.S. member. "Our lady of *love!*"

"Oh, *darling!*" cried another, "Make me thine and thine alone, forever!"

Yet another chimed in, "For thee, my beloved, have I saved myself—for thee, and no one else!"

"Star of stars!"

"Dream of dreams!"

"Rapture of raptures!"

"Here be the dragon's head!" declared one donning a suit of aluminum foil armor; and at his declaration, he cast at her feet the recently severed head of a chicken. "Come away with me, princess! And let us together discover and take our fill of *TRUE LOVE!*"

At this, a group of female M.O.S.Q.U.I.T.O.E.S. released the crazed body of the decapitated fowl and formed an impenetrable circle around Adeline. Blood pulsed through the air, drenching the petrified and crying Adeline, and streaking across the manic and laughing faces of the M.O.S.Q.U.I.T.O.E.S. horde, until at long last the chicken fell motionless and the crowd disbanded, leaving Adeline in the courtyard to tremble and weep in a pool of crimson beside a butchered fowl.

***

True Love.

Adeline sat shivering in the shower, there, still fully-clothed, with her legs to her chest, as the frigid rain poured over her fragile skin and stained rags.

Her world had ever believed in Love, True Love; but the *real* world knew it by a different name, and not at all—of this she was now aware and at last certain.

What was this Love, she wondered, that had once been and was no more?

When did come this Magic of sensual pleasures to replace the Love of old?

Where had all the believers gone, the ones who'd sought

after Love?

Who could have guessed that Love could prove so insufficient?

Why was Love not enough?

And how could she have been so easily deceived into believing that Love had lain in so wayward a heart?

A million more lines of inquiry were exhausted before her fingertips began to turn blue.

Examining herself, she found the chicken's blood had not yet been washed away.

Her quaking hand reached for the faucet.

Having stopped the rain, she fell onto her face and coiled into a ball.

The tears that pooled warmed her skin.

And in them ran the blood that had stained.

***

True Love.

She lay there for a span outside of time.

How sure she had been.

How foolish, now, did she find herself.

Her wet skin and soaked rags dried ever so slowly.

She did not stir until every icy droplet and cooling tear had been lifted into the air.

Love—she had been *so* sure.

How could a heart so full of the stuff had been wrong?

It *was* Magic, what they'd had. This, in her heart, she knew for certain.

But, perhaps, the reality was that they'd never had anything at all.

What she'd felt: was it Love?

She searched her heart, searched her mind, searched her hands.

Empty, all of them.

No, she thought.

No, she feared.

She had never had Love.

She had never held Love.

She had never known Love.

She had never felt Love.

Never.

Never.

Not once.

***

True Love.

Again she searched her hands.

Never had, never held, never known, and never truly felt but a phantom.

And never *made*.

This word paired with Love was an odd phrase: a combination used to neuter speech. Of course, she knew its popular intent; but it struck her, just now, as the tub entered bone-dry territory, that perhaps this was yet another element of the Love of old that had by time been cast into misinterpretation. Perhaps, to *make*, in the real sense, meant something far different than its current, carnal implication described. Perhaps, thought she, lifting her ratty, partially dried head, and staring intently through the open door and down the hall, Love was indeed a product of careful crafting—yes, thought she: the phrase, if it were to be found true to the original intent behind the articulation of this aspect of Love, would need a rewording. To have; to hold; to know, to feel…and to *craft* Love…to *forge* Love…to *create* Love…to build it, fashion it, assemble it, construct it.

Love, it seemed—that Love of old—required a little elbow grease.

And so came the question: How is Love crafted?

What *is* Love?

The latter query, which she had never until this day pondered, had become secondary to the former.

Craft it, and see.

Adeline rose from the tub.

***

When Adeline returned to school, she found that the interest in her had faded. This could perhaps be due to her time away—but for how long was she away? She could not tell, nor could she draw from any indications found at school. Homework was always a bad indicator, as students had after much persuasion succeeded in convincing the administration that assigned work could infect in a pupil "negative" Magic, causing their own Magic to suffer to such a degree as to require counseling, for which Enderbrine's was not about to pay. So, all students worked post-class as they pleased, arriving by his or her own pace and workload at the same destination as the rest of the students. (Negative Magic, you see, had also been detected in academic scorings

and rankings, as well as in merits and even graduations. Such ceremonies, and the diplomas distributed thereat, were no longer exclusive to an elite few: those who'd at least met what were now outdated, violent, exclusionary, and oppressive minimum requirements. Fairness and balance was at last achieved, and the bar that had once been used for setting was never seen again).

Anyway, Adeline returned to a place operating ever as it had done, with no sign that a step had been missed along the way.

Singleness was boring to M.O.S.Q.U.I.T.O.E.S., unless one was the coveted cover model of Enderbrine's *Magic Enders* Magazine (Enders being short for Enderbriners). From among the herd of Enders, the administration would select a student they felt fit (or, could fit) the desired trend of the week, then hurl them into a makeup chair, and go to work transforming them into the face of the school. And, during that week, there was naught but the cover of *ME*. He or she was the most admired and well-known pupil, hoisted high on shoulders donning the same robes as said student had worn during the magazine photo shoot; high-fives were distributed left and right, praise was showered, and extra pudding cups from the cafeteria were reverently bestowed; fingers and toes were kissed, photos were snapped at every turn, bright flashes blinding the way; hair was caressed and locks were yanked for souvenirs; patches of clothing were torn and sold, fists were thrown whenever the smiles dimmed, bones were broken when the strut became trite and annoying, and blood was taken to satisfy the eternally obsessed, as well as the jealous mob in need of a step by which to gain better altitude.

If ever your better judgment fails you and you find yourself roaming about the school of enchantment, keep an eye on its hallway corners—you just might catch a glimpse of a former *ME* cover model laid up inside.

But, Adeline was now single. Adam had moved on to other women, and there was nothing more to be said. The jokes that had taken down the house and Adeline's sense of self-worth had gone stale and had since been replaced by better models. She was as much an outsider as the bloodied and tattered heaps of mangled flesh stuffed in the corners she passed on her way to class.

And, with this, she had no objection.

***

"Magic is a limitless thing—boundless, infinite, immeasurable, inexhaustible; and, most importantly, completely fathomless."

Most students heard words like the ones spoken on this day as would the subjects of subliminal messaging tests: indirectly, though with a lasting practical effect. Eyes and fingers preoccupied with his or her own urgent task of the moment, or everyday addiction, idle brains acted as adhesive paper to the words drifting through the classroom. This group was what the prevailing mass or authority made them to be; and what an immense joy for the teachers of Enderbrine's to have such a collection of students saved from the voices of those who spoke of false, dangerous Magic! Wisdom like the brand brewed for and shared among Enderbrine's teaching staff had an obligation to be inserted into the delicate vessels before them, lest they be not true Enders.

"Know yourself, and you will know it. Seek deep within, and

you will find it. Reach deeply; touch it. Listen as it whispers; feel it. Employ its teachings; experience it. For what you hear, what you feel—these are natural things; and there is no flaw in the grand, adventitious design of nature."

Another group participated actively, building upon the words and works of their instructors—using only the words and works spoken and demonstrated, and nothing else—to form their own, unique metamorphosis. With such a learned Magical foundation as was their paid masters and mistresses, they were made confident in their guided discoveries and pre-digested understandings; their re-revelations and implanted individuality made them the pride and joy of the school.

"Magic cannot be suppressed. It cannot be tamed. It cannot be measured, exhausted, or expired. And it cannot be fully comprehended without the proper instruction. Magic is simply what it is, and can be defined only by the one in whom it exists."

And then there were the students who asked, "Why?"

These were quickly expelled.

"But if you put these things into practice, if you really take the time and invest heavily into yourself—what you dream, what you feel, what you most desperately want: these will be added unto you, and you will indeed be what you dream, what you feel, and what you want."

Adeline was this day found not in any of these groups. Once a member of group A, the first mentioned, she now participated as a party of one, somewhere between groups B and C. And it was the collection of words presented in the latter paragraph that had been her calling out into a new classification, and the words below her release into the practice thereof.

"Class dismissed."

***

"Know yourself."

Step one.

"Know yourself."

Do so, and true Magic will also be known.

And in so knowing, her dreams, her feelings, her desires—all these would be added unto her.

So, what did she dream?

Easy: True Love. She dreamt of True Love.

What did she feel?

Easier still: That True Love would conquer all the negative Magic dwelling within, which forbade the Magical happiness wrought of the very thing of which she dreamt.

And what did she want? What was her great desire?

That was the easiest of them all: To be the exclusive recipient of one person's True Love…and to have that person be Adam.

It was time now to put the teachings of Enderbrine's into practice and take a dive into herself, there to find the key to securing the elusive heart that would fill the void in her own.

She knew Magic lay somewhere inside of her—but where, exactly?

All these things she pondered whilst putting on her face in the morning.

And that's when it hit her.

The mirror suddenly became detached from the wall and hit her squarely in the forehead.

Luckily, it had maintained its integrity and did not shatter into a million pieces—more than that, it lead to an inspiration.

As she grumbled through gritted teeth and sore skull, dabbing the pronounced bump with a concealer from Enderbrine's Mystical Maquillage Kit (a standard-issue makeup set distributed to all first-year females), she saw clearly a bit of Magic that had proven rather effective in stealing glances, dropping jaws, and causing not a few bodies attached to turned heads to walk directly into opened locker doors or tumble down flights of stairs (doors and stairs which, thought the formerly turned and now bruised heads when the concussion shock had finally passed, had surely sprouted out of thin air—'twas, after all, a school of Magic, was it not?).

And what was this Magic?

Why, 'twas Beauty, of course!

Now, Adeline thought not the Magic of Beauty was particularly potent within her: a sentiment reinforced by the Mystical Maquillage Kit she'd received on day one. Throughout her awakening into self-awareness, she had endeavored to strengthen by whatever means necessary that which was in her eyes an obvious weakness; but, until acquiring the Mystical Maquillage Kit, the results had been mediocre, at best. Sure, she'd stolen a glance or two; but not one had ever led to a friendly "Hello," or an invitation to share a beverage and a conversation—not until the employment of Enderbrinian Magic.

Yes, this kit, its Magical contents, had offered her many eager salutations and invitations for the fielding. And how wonderful it had felt to have options! What great and awesome power to be handed someone's cup and choose whether to fill it, return it, or cast it down to be shattered. The latter was not her bag, whatsoever; nor was she one to pour samples into waiting cups. Returning had been her intoxicating habit, made all the more exhilarating by the fact that she so desired to find the perfect cup and into it pour her everything. She had seen how content and satisfied waiting cups had been to receive drops and dashes from the streams of her female peers, only for those sample-seeking recipients, now with the memory of the taste wet on their lips, to thereafter loose some or all enthusiasm in said stream.

This, she had been determined, would never be the case for her. And, so, though terribly difficult and seemingly impossible for a party of one to do, she persisted: a lone stream, knowing no banks, flowing with increasing speed and pressure, ever as if her waters had just broken free of a dam, toward that one, special cup she knew lay just around the next bend. Though, it must be noted, that the word "bend" should be used loosely and in only a short span of her history of flowing; for, as time went on, time that was to her far more protracted than that which was told by the spinning earth, what were once bends had become a broad beeline. And so great and sure had become the power of her flow, thought she in this present moment, that she had, perhaps, emptied too hastily.

No.

It had been carelessness.

Indeed, it had been!

Adam was—*is*…well, I mean, have you *seen* him?

A most desired cup!

To be offered *that* cup was to be offered…well, paradise, I suppose.

And, she continued, had not she become careless and comfortable, believing for a second one could relax one's wielding of the powerful Magic of Beauty, his cup could never have been filled with anything more appealing or delightful than she—and the taste of waters past would have been expelled as drops of oil before rushing waves!

A chance had been given, and she'd blown it.

But all of that was about to change.

Casting a determined eye into the mirror, she set in motion the renovation of her face beneath the mighty arm of Beauty Magic.

Dabbing here and there with this and that, brushing up and down, smearing to and fro; fluffing and spritzing and combing and painting and coating and puffing and powdering; poking and prodding, pulling and cutting—if the verb could be suffixed with an "–ing," she did it.

Finally, after hours upon hours of brewing a potent brew for her face, she waltzed confidently into her closet to pick out a wrapping in which to wrap herself. Unfortunately, nothing particularly striking hung there for the taking, nor did any of the options feel like the proper size. So, she consulted for further instruction one of Enderbrine's most-read and ever-updating book of Magic: *ME Magazine*.

After an intense study thereof, she had successfully *abracadabra*-ed the contents of her refrigerator and pantry to disappear, along with all the cash in her wallet; and from this cauldron emerged a rippling, red dress and a slender waistline to slip beneath it.

The product of this brew was nearly ideal—just a bit too sickly; not exactly the sylphlike figure the batch had promised. So, she restocked the fridge and pantry with foods that had had their flavors cursed, and submitted herself to a rigorous regiment, daily calling down upon her body violent hexes of fiery pain, all through perhaps the most sluggish form of Magic:

Deadweight Levitation.

Eventually, she beheld in her Magic mirror a face she did not recognize, but in which she held great confidence, set atop a frame formed from much Magical labor and wrapped neatly in a delightfully garish red dress.

It had been quite a brew, but *this* batch of Beauty Magic, thought she, was one for the books.

She was ready.

What day was it? How long had she been away?

As before and once again, it didn't matter.

She was back, and back in red: a steal-your-eye kind of red, painted ever so elegantly over and punctuating the ensemble that walked amid a cloud of the sweetest fragrances, sure to fill the nostrils and drain the cranial domes of passersby: rather a make-your-legs-into-wet-spaghetti-as-I-walk-by kind of appearance. Her body, however, trembled all the way to the school doors—violent tremors, for she was not used to what she might become among the waiting crowd, nor had her body yet given up reminding her how much it preferred life with a fully-stocked refrigerator, busting at the seams with flavorful foods. But Beauty Magic had ever been said to bear within it a bolstering effect; and on this she relied to carry her through to the prize.

And, so, she entered the school.

Her Magic mirror had taught and had helped her perfect a strut, as well as a face to go along with it. The *click* of her heels matched the pace of the eager hearts by which she passed, though her pace was perceived as if the air through which she did glide was a crystal clear ocean, teasing the ends of her hair like a lazy, warm breeze, and trapping her body in slow motion;

and her piercing stare, perched like a morning mist above her pursed and equally well-attired lips, brought each heart and wayward wanderer to a screeching halt.

Click-clack she did through the growing crowd, all the while absorbing the rushing weight of a thousand eyes. Her trembling body became more and more relaxed with every soothing wave of realization that she was safe in the gaze of the hungry horde. A real smoothness soon entered her stride, and she became totally at ease—how natural it felt to don the skin of tempting prey and waltz among the wolves, all aching to devour, while to her they presented their necks for leashing. The howling pack showered her with palpable attention; however, this was but a tickling sensation, for the true, all-consuming prize lay just ahead.

"Hello, Adam."

"Hey, Beautif—"

BLAM

Now, while you, dear reader, might have set up this scene in your mind as a moment of sweet revenge, in which Adeline dons some empowerment and becomes the envy of all the school, before finding the boy who had scorned her, and then knocking him one in the nose (a supposition just now validated by the all-caps *BLAM*), I must poke a pin in that bubble.

Though she had been working out and was presently sporting what those in the weightlifting community might in technical terms refer to as "baby boulder shoulders," Adeline's punch had not yet graduated to the level of *BLAM*. Rather, hers would be best described as a *BOP*—still, nothing at which to shake a stick (because, why shake a stick at anything? Turn up your nose, or refuse to write home to the family about the experience, if you want to make a coherent point about being unimpressed); but it was something, nonetheless. A few more triceps exercises, and she'd be in *BLAM* territory.

Despite this update on her pummeling prowess, I must direct you to the reality that no punches had been thrown from either party—and I make this point to address both parties just in case you, dear reader, might have thought the shell shock of having been body slammed by this very girl some indeterminate time ago had potentially brought forth from Adam a reflexive swing of self-defense.

So, whence came this *BLAM?* What was its source?

Well, credit him as you will, Adam saw what no eye had yet perceived: Adeline.

You see, no eye beholding her on her way to the object of her intent had recognized the girl beneath the painted mask— nor had Adam, for that matter, until, mid-reply, he turned and, in a fraction of a second, beheld that wave in her eyes: that lost and wild wave, slamming against the mighty stone.

Then only did he know her.

And, thus, was he, as if compelled by the sudden burst of a violent wind, *BLAM*-ed up against the lockers.

"*Adeline?*"

"Hi."

At least, that's what she had wanted to say.

No words came in that moment.

She was utterly lost in his astounded gaze, wondering what on earth it could mean.

Was he overwhelmed by Beauty?

Did he find her hideous?

Had she approached too suddenly, startling him and ruining

the moment? (There were definitely some glaring context clues for this one).

Was he guessing when he'd said her name?

Did he really not recognize her?

Her mind was so flooded with a zillion more questions and trails of thought that she missed whatever sounds had preceded his suddenly saying, "Well, I guess I'll see you around," which he thereafter followed up with a sharp spinning on his heels to make his way in the opposite direction.

Snapping back into the present, she quickly turned to see him walking down the hall, his arm draped over another girl. And, without thinking, she called breathlessly after him.

"I'M BEAUTIFUL!"

"You've got *that* right," he said, gazing at the girl under his arm as he walked.

"I've got *everything* right," the girl replied, and then nuzzled her head into his shoulder, as another girl inserted herself beneath his other, welcoming arm.

It was then, as Adeline's mask began to melt beneath a waterfall pouring forth from her eyes, and her body fell against the lockers and dropped to the floor, that the world at last came into focus; and she saw the crowds cluttering the halls, lined with hooting, excited boys ogling at girls who looked as though they had strutted right out of her own Magic mirror.

Eventually, a bell rang and the halls emptied; and she, after a time that nearly took her to the next bell, rose and began a slumped slink through the desolate space.

"How they treating *you*?" came a hoarse and laboring voice from somewhere below.

Adeline hardly had the strength or will to turn her head; but she did so, and there beheld a young girl, perhaps a year or two older than she, curled up in a corner: her face was dirty, her eyes red and heavy; both heels were tattered and chipped, the sparkling red dress she wore barely sparkled and was more a marshy-maroon shade, with tears along every seam through which her wasting body had protruded. Her hair was mangled, her teeth rotting, and she wobbled something fierce, fighting what looked like crippling weakness, propping her body up on the one arm that wasn't twisted or withered, that she might elevate her lips high enough to be heard.

But she didn't stop or slow her pace, Adeline.

She said not a word.

She just continued on her way, returning her head to its hung position, and rounded the curves and corners until at last she was home, sobbing over a pint of ice cream.

***

Beauty.

What worthless Magic, thought she!

Here today and gone tomorrow: this was Beauty: a fleeting spell that remained constant only in eyes deceived by the toils of the potion's brewing!

She felt she had not the strength required to maintain a level of potency in her Beauty brew that would hex her beloved enough to yield a consistent desired effect through an ever after—but, even this was not the real issue: Adam's response to the spell had been like that of a child who is served the same sweet, strawberry treat for the hundredth day in a row, or who receives as a gift the same shiny toy truck, year after year: Bored.

Been there, done that; seen it before; familiar with that brew—was good, but who doesn't have it?

Adeline had surely served up a brew powerful enough to level any living creature—or, at least, it might have done so at one time. Among her peers, her brew was seen as common. The prospect potentially lying behind the skin of the offering had called forth the beating hearts and dangling jaws; but these followed her only so long as it took to realize hers was show only and no tell. The tellers were the prize, and used like paper straws to sup a drop of sparkling delight, before being relegated to the corners of Enderbrine's endless, filthy, forsaken halls, flattened and used.

So, if Beauty was not enough to tempt the heart of Adam back to its destiny, what might she add to the brew that would elevate her above the rest?

Fate—or, so it seemed—would step in to lend an answer to this query.

At midday, on yet another lonely weekend, when at last the morning tears had flowed and their beds were dry, Adeline heard from her opened window the sound of a young and cheerful bluebird, singing its third song since the day of its hatching (though, she was unaware of this last detail—such are privy only to we in the profession of Narratorial Omniscience, and those with whom we would share such information).

Oh, how sweet and innocent was this song! With verses devoted to the newness of air filling its lungs, the exhilarating power of wind rushing beneath its wings, and glorious, life-giving light to bring forth all the world to its eyes; a chorus praising the miracle that was its own existence, the joy and mystery of being alive; and a hopeful bridge in its midst, the grandest of the elements, chirping long and ever so loudly, on notes high and soaring with grace and strength, telling of an overwhelming desire to break free of its benevolent, blessed nest and ascend into the endless masterpiece of clouds, tumble through the playful breeze, and dance—oh, glory, yes; dance!—among the burgeoning splendor, the magnificent scope of which it could but imagine!

How grand a world must lie beyond, it seemed to say, and what in it might *I* be?

Thoroughly inspired, Adeline rushed to her pantry and collected a handful of seeds. Sprinting with these back to her window, she lined the sill with the banquet and called the baby bird to hop from its nest and eat.

It was a perilous journey from nest to sill, having to trot carefully along a thin and wind-tossed branch to a slab of painted wood, all set ever so high above a meadow of green, faded into watercolor by the great distance. But, after a short time and struggle, the bird made it to the sill; and with every bite of the bounteous buffet of mixed harvest, it sang a glorious tune of thanks to the majestic creature in the mighty tree beside its own. This song Adeline eagerly captured into a mixture of honey, lemon, and hot water—the final ingredient in a potion called Song.

Thankfully, the exertive pursuit of Beauty had given her a leg-up (or, perhaps, *lung*-up would here be more appropriate) in brewing a potent potion, providing tremendous air support with which to wield the tonic once it had been ingested; for Song was a complex bit of Magic, and she wasn't all too convinced that her swiping at the air through which the bluebird's song had flowed, trying to direct the sound waves into her brew pot, had actually worked, as the spellbook had claimed it would. She even set the next line of seeds on the part of the sill inside her room, so as to limit any outdoor interference from stealing the precious song as the bird trustingly waltzed forth, blithely nibbling.

She had hoped the bird would eat and sing a little more; but so small was the bird that its fill was had rather quickly.

Bowing (or, so she'd perceived), the bird bounced back to its nest, and there drifted to sleep, where it would dream of the days to come, when the generous meal it had eaten would spread wide its wings and let it soar at last and forevermore.

Adeline watched, a little disappointedly, as the bird hopped away, leaving a line of seeds uneaten in her room. With a sigh, she shut the window and made for the cellar, where she would begin the careful combining of Beauty and Song: a pair of potent Magical spells sure to win the heart of Adam.

She worked all through the night and into the morn, until she had a brew with which she was rather confident—the mirror had survived her glance without a crack and the walls had echoed well their approval; it was time to test her work on the living. And what better creature on which to lay the first sample than the bird whose song she had borrowed to make herself sing?

Though incredibly tired, she darted up the stairs as the sun began to dawn and threw open the window to see the bird.

But it was gone.

A single feather had been left behind in the nest.

It seemed its dream had come true.

It was now high above the clouds, admiring all the eye could see and wondering what part something of its insignificant size and ability had to play in a world so vast and wonderful as this one.

Adeline gave a small smile and wished the bird well, as she sealed her window and plopped down into her bed to rest from the toils of the night.

She slept deeply and long, expiring the last hours of the weekend in dreams, where she sang in tune with the bluebird, perched atop her shoulder, to tremendous awe and admiration from a crowd that stretched far and wide before her.

Song.

What powerful, freeing Magic!

And hers was good—*very* good.

Even among billions of faces, she could see Adam's; and painted upon it was that same awe and admiration, but also adoration and desperate Love.

She had done it.

At last, she—

BANG!

Shooting bolt upright in bed, Adeline looked frantically about the room.

Had she slept for a whole day?

Or, was it but an hour?

And then she remembered.

School!

What time was it?

OH NO!

She'd missed first period! She'd missed the morning rush, when she could have displayed her Song for a million adoring eyes, becoming their envy, and there within Adam spur a jealousy so great he would see every eye gouged out and cast into the dust, that he alone might gaze upon her and absorb her magnificent performance!

Leaping from her bed, she took a giant swig of her Beauty and Song brew, and like a whirling tornado sped through her house, dressing and gathering all she needed for the day.

With a quick glance into the mirror, she saw that the Beauty was just as potent as it had been the other day; and with a few *tra-la-la*s hurled into the house's most acoustically friendly places, she fortified her confidence in the Song.

Taking in a deep breath, she set her strut into motion and glided out to win the heart of Adam. And as the door slammed behind her, the alarm clock on her nightstand began to buzz—and buzz it did, until it crashed to the floor, there to rattle and scream a muffled scream until eventually throwing in the towel, wearied by the blatant disregard for the fruit of its labor.

There seemed to be an awful lot of commotion in the courtyard for second period. She had never known her fellow pupils to gather and lounge about in the time between classes—but, then again, she, personally and seemingly exclusively, had always found Punctuality to be a most enriching Magic. It was not uncommon to find students disregarding the loosely to not-at-all-enforced laws of class times in order to take in a little recreation here and there. But, still, *this* kind of a crowd was most unusual for this time of day. Perhaps, thought she, today was some sort of on-campus holiday, of which she had yet heard nothing. Such would make sense, surely; for her attendance record had been spotty as of late. Indeed, something special must have been afoot on this warm and windy day. And, whatever it was, it would soon pale in comparison to the spectacle she was about to become.

Adeline, who had been anxiously watching the crowd from the nearby bushes stepped forth now to bring down the house with a rockin' tune. But no sooner had she lifted herself from behind the bushy veil did a sudden realization knock her square in the chest and send her squatting down again: Waltzing through the halls was one thing—but setting oneself upon a stage?

This she had neglected to consider.

While she had belted many a fearless note in the shower at home, and reenacted with histrionic vim scenes from her favorite books or movies to an audience of stuffed animals, who filled her head with thunderous applause every time, she was not the type to translate these things into the *real* world, the one in which blink eyes of unknown judgments and censures, the one that bore the risks of failure and humiliation. She rarely even volunteered answers in class, unless she was certain her words were infallible, regardless of the school's supposed spell of Universal Approval, which Magically made every opinion and answer the right one. (Oh, how many times the world must have been drastically altered within a thirty second span, day in and day out!).

But, Beauty—did this not have that bolstering effect? Was it not also a spell in which was found boldness for the wielder?

She wondered whether it would be wise to doubt the very thing in which she had invested so much time and energy; but, given the paralyzing quakes that suddenly began to entrap her body, perhaps Beauty had a fleeting potency after all—or, maybe she had misapplied it in her haste that morning. Either way, she could not raise herself to approach the crowd, much less do any kind of public display of Song.

This, however, could not quell her determination.

She was Magical, was she not?

Something could be done.

Rifling through her bag, she clasped her hands down upon the Magical potions book *Stir to Spur: Blend and Brew a Better You!*

Flipping through the pages, she found the desired recipe: *Confidence.*

The first ingredient was Phlegm.

"Well," thought she, "it's not very ladylike; but, eyes on the prize, I suppose."

With a snort and a hack, a gurgle, and a few hems, she expelled a thick, warm, and terribly slimy bit of murky white, in which swam a hint of lime; it fell quickly into her handy pocket-sized cauldron with a nauseating *SPLAT.* Fighting the urge to hurl and, after some difficulty, severing from her tonsils the reluctant tail of the foul first ingredient, she moved on to ingredient number two: Mettle.

She had never seen *metal* spelled this way. It was an old book, though—perhaps old-timey people used not to know how to spell things in a practical matter, thought she.

Now, where could she get some metal?

After looking around for a bit, she remembered that once when she was a child a tooth had by a clump of metal been Magically repaired. Her mother, as she recalled, had been rather disappointed that the Tooth Wizard from the land of Fluorince, and his fairy assistant, had had to perform such Magic in the first place. Adeline, however, could not have been happier, and was to the present puzzled over her mother's disappointment;

for Adeline had always believed her mouth cursed until that Magical metal had been set in place. Her youth had been blessed with a wonderful set of pearly whites; but these quickly began to fall freely from her gums, and she knew not why. Bigger, uglier models took their places; however, they seemed hexed with a spell of Churlishness, for they warred painfully over the limited space in her mouth. The Tooth Wizard had tamed them with a series of metal wires; and, though they fought and wailed against the Magic, they were eventually subdued. And then, they began to rot—but this wad of Magical metal had saved the day. Once it had been placed over a rotting tooth, peace reigned in her mouth.

This metal would undoubtedly be the best for such a brew as this.

So, carefully, she scraped and picked at it with her nail, trying to get just a sliver of the metal, as she feared extracting the whole thing might send her mouth once more into chaos.

Eventually, she got her sliver.

Placing this into the cauldron, she looked to ingredient number three: Nerve.

She would like attaining this one far less than she had the phlegm.

Looking around again, she saw many creatures scurrying about the wind-tossed space. A squirrel dashed across the green and up a tree, where it caught sight of a friend and made playful chase, round and round.

Nope.

She couldn't do it.

How about an insect?

A beetle walked along the border between sidewalk and

grass, appearing intent on catching for a midday snack one of the many leaves tumbling about in the blustery wind.

Gross.

Not doing it.

Just then she heard the school bell ring.

Peeking out from behind the bush, she saw many of the students shuffling about and through the doors.

Another opportunity had passed.

Oh, well; she hadn't been prepared.

Her brew was not yet brewed.

But that posed another problem: Time.

Because she had gotten such a late start, the whole day could end before she'd gotten herself ready; and the more the hours ticked, the less likely was she to discover an audience waiting for her. The student population dwindled rapidly as the day progressed, and practically none of the remaining lingered following the final bell. Even worse, she had no idea where Adam might be at a given time—student privilege allowed individuals to break from his or her set schedule and attend whatever class so pleased them. Adam could have been anywhere.

Freezing Time would have been ideal, but such a spell was considered advanced Magic; and those who tried were often left disfigured, with giant lips and skin pulled ever so thinly back across the skull, as if the flesh were trying to burrow into the ears. Those who'd endeavored to stop Time's relentless pace were painfully obvious to onlookers; yet, they were a curiously ignorant, oblivious bunch, as far as the effects of their failed attempts are concerned; and this ignorance led them again and again to those dark cauldrons: the long, cylindrical ones, filled with potent potions funneled through needles, that could bring great light, yet were known mostly for the intensity of the blackness they could produce.

No.

Freezing Time was too risky.

But, perhaps she could slow it down a bit.

Setting aside *Stir to Spur*, she fumbled about for another text.

Good Enough: Simple Spells to Get You By in a Pinch

Adeline had found this title at a local discount bookshop. Though it appeared to have been well used by its surely many previous owners, every page was accounted for and the cover was intact—it even bore still the star-like sticker stamped on it when it was brand new, reading, "So Easy, They Just Might Work!"

Thumbing through the time-stained pages, she at last came upon *O'Clock, O'Stop.*

Clever, no doubt, whoever had named these spells.

As with every spell nuzzled between the covers, this one was straightforward and simple: Recite incantation; preform action; get results.

"O Me! O My!" she began in a sharp cry, that quickly became aware of itself and faded hastily into a whisper—this, however, was soon lost in a rush of mighty gusts of wind that sent her hair into a whirl and pounded against her body with tremendous force, filling her to the brim with a surge of great power, until her voice morphed into a bellowing howl.

"O Me! O My!" she began again. "Two hands! One eye! Round and round—*Alas*! You're done! Entrap the Moon! Stop the Sun! Blind the eye! And for the hands a molasses bath! Command I now your endless pace to slow! Be still! Be still, 'til I say *GO!*"

And, as if by Magic, the whirling winds suddenly stopped.

Adeline, who had in the rush of the moment sealed her eyes and cast her fists to the heavens, slowly peeled back the veil and saw that the world was at peace—even the beetle had at last caught a leaf, and was presently perched atop it, perfectly still, as if carefully pondering which end it would eat first.

The earth's rotation, Time itself, had been halted, no doubt—or, at least, slowed, for gentle wisps yet danced by her every now and then.

With a contented sigh, she rose and made for the local market. There she located the Mage of Meats, and asked if he had any nerve he could sell.

Happy to oblige, and moving about rather speedily for one trapped in slowed Time (perhaps, thought she, Time alone had been made sluggish, leaving all others unaffected—*Magically*, of course), the Mage took a gob from the nervous system of the day's fresh cut and plopped it into the cauldron that Adeline held at as great a length as she could manage, with her head turned and eyes squeezed shut.

Three ingredients down, one to go: Aplomb.

Again, those old-timers and their spelling! This time, they couldn't even be bothered to separate the indefinite article from the noun! (She didn't use those *exact* terms—rather, her words went as follows: *They couldn't even bother to put a space between the mini word and the bigger word!*). How ridiculous, thought she! How lazy! And when was it ever acceptable to spell *plum* as *plomb*?

Maybe it was a typo?

Whatever the issue, a plum would be easy enough to find, now that she was in the market. And, procuring one, she tossed it into the mix and began to stir.

Not much happened.

There was no fizzing or sizzling.

No bubbling or boiling.

All this toil and trouble, and not so much as a bubble!

Oh, well.

Sometimes Magic is not so showy, I guess.

Nor, in this case, did it turn out to be pleasant.

Though her lips were more than a little reluctant to separate, she lifted to her trembling mouth a concoction of ingredients seemingly determined to oppose one another and never join as one; and with a tight pinching of the nose and a painfully tight squeezing of the eyes, she threw back the slimy, lumpy, sharp, warm, and runny concoction, aiming to send it sailing directly past the tongue and down through the esophagus to be processed into Magic.

But her throat, adroitly detecting the madness long before its gates were breeched, sealed with impressive speed the port to the pit, leaving the potion no recourse other than to crash against her tonsils, exploding like a tempest-tossed wave slamming against a towering, rocky cliff, before hastily rebounding and flooding her mouth.

Like a bucket of spilled paint over a priceless sculpture, the foul mixture coated her tongue; but, given the trouble she had endured to make this potion, and given her need for its promised results, she, very much against her will, closed off any escape through her lips, causing the sloshing mixture to surge to and fro through every crevice of her mouth, ensuring she tasted it—all of it, and the vomit that soon joined it—to the fullest extent. Her eyes darted about for some sort of aid—water; or, maybe a handful of leaves might mask (or, with their own tang) distract from the taste.

The insanity soon ended with an audible *GULP*, followed by a great many desperate gasps and laudable heaving forbiddances, her quaking frame kneeling beside and with a steadying hand atop the curb. But every moment she suffered ended with a greater feeling of revival and strength than the one preceding it; and soon she was standing tall on her own two feet, her chest fully elevated, head held high with her arms outstretched to the clouds; and as her watering eyes sealed and the wind began to collect and grow stronger, spiraling up her legs and torso until it was blowing with a force greater than it had all day, sending her long, sunny hair into a frenzy, she hollered at the tippy top of her lungs, "GO!"

Time had been released from its restraints, the earth resumed its spinning—and, boy, did it spin! Adeline found it rather difficult to walk back to the school, what with the whipping winds and the supersonic merry-go-round effect caused by the earth making up for the spins it had missed; her head was a dizzy daze of disorientation until her hand fell against the solid structure of Enderbrine's. Once inside and feeling more adjusted to the earth's pace, she looked around for a clock.

Noon.

What a success the *O'Clock, O'Stop* spell had been!

Her time gathering the potion ingredients would surely have taken nearly half the school day had not the clock been slowed! Here, a mere *two* classes had run their courses; and now was placed at her feet a prime time for exercising her brewed Confidence for all to see.

Still, even with all the extra *ticks* and *tocks* she'd acquired, there was not one she could afford to waste, for who could tell just how long Confidence would last?

Adeline sprinted at full speed down the halls, rounding corners with such haste it blew over the dwellers therein; whizzing past hall monitors—"Mind the safety of others!" one shouted, before hastily following up with, "But don't let that rob you of the Magic found in your freedom to be the best of who and what you are!"

Another hollered, "Slow down!" and then quickly added, "If it does your Magic well, that is—otherwise, *GO, GO, GO!*"

A few wide-open barricades later, she found herself in the lunchroom; and, leaping onto a thinly populated table (mostly accommodating the disciples and social descendants of the formally-named Harry Oliver), she let out a triumphant bellow, announcing her arrival, that turned every head and laid a thick blanket of silence over the crowd.

She savored but a moment of the power Confidence had wrought from the cowardice that had ever lurked in her heart; and, parting her lips, she cast forth her Song.

"*I guess you're pretty,*" she began, taking up a chicken drumstick from a student's plate beside her foot and singing into it, as if it were a microphone; her extended finger parted the mass before her, snatching Adam from the crowd.

"*I guess you're smart,*" she continued; these words were not her own, but were rather a well-known, chart-topping hit from the previous summer.

"*I guess you've taken hold of my heart.*"

A most romantic song: thusly had it been hailed; and she sang every note to perfection, her voice gliding like a gentle river over smooth stones in its path.

"*I guess I've never felt this way before,*" she purred; and then, as with the mouth of a tornado, she sucked in a great gulp of air and belted the next line: "*I guess I'd* DIE *if you walked out the door!*"

Oh, the ease, control, and power with which she hit that high note! The crowd could not help but leap to its feet in a roar of applause.

"*I guess one day,*" came a raspy, grungy, really rock 'n' roll kind of sound that set the lunchroom on fire, "*I'll learn what this is all about.*"

Chaotic whooping and hollering filled the room, while a great many students excitedly filled their chests to join in for the final lines.

Sealing her eyes and throwing back her head, her hair streaking through the air in a perfect, half-moon arc, like a bolt of yellow lightning, Adeline cried above the din, "*I GUESS I'M IN LOVE!*"

And, whipping forward her head and sunny locks, she readied to unleash the final line, her eyes fixed on Adam's adoring face, there to slam the closing, Love-sealing words against his helpless body, and like a fish on a line draw him forth to the table on which she stood, extracting from the crowded pond this rarest of catches, that they might swim for the rest of their days in an aquarium all their own, away from all other hooks and lines and lures.

"*I GUESS I'LL FIND OUT!*"

Yes, indeed!

How explosive were those words!

Though, Adeline had muttered only the words "I guess;" the rowdy student body had bellowed the rest, and had started a frenzied encore, oblivious to her.

She, likewise, was oblivious to them; for, there, just ahead, where an adoring fish should have been caught helplessly on a line being reeled to her side for the swift commencement of a happily ever after, she found a fish dancing between two other fishes, their own lines coiled about him. And they were all singing, cheering, screaming the tune that had been hurled into their wild hearts.

Something was not right.

Had Song failed?

Given the student body's present state of manic singing, it would seem everyone had been affected by the Magic; yet, while Adam did also sing along with his female partners, he appeared more amused by Dance.

But, Adeline had not prepared Dance Magic. And this moment, thought she, was poised to start rapidly slipping away from her; so, she improvised.

Leaping from the table, she rushed over to Adam and began to mimic the actions of the girls amusing him, hoping also that their Dance Magic might bleed over to her, as her Song had bled into them.

But though she wiggled and twisted until she was gasping for breath and sweating profusely, his attention would not detach from the moment and fix solely upon her. Sure, she received from him the occasional, heart-jolting glance of desire; but it was the same one he threw about to all the girls flocking to him like scraps of metal to a magnet.

Eventually, the crowd had drunk its fill of Song, and one by one they departed, high-fiving and sharing in the residual jovialities gleaned from the rare moment they would remember no more once the start of the next five minutes waiting in the offing had arrived.

And Adam, as before, departed with a girl under each arm—not the same girls as the time prior, but each arm was occupied, nonetheless. He had, however, offered Adeline one of those spots; but it was obvious that she was in no way special to his eyes in that moment. And, so, exhausted and kneeling on the marble floor, she turned away from Adam's extended hand and would not watch as he walked off toward some other wherever.

It was rather late when she finally returned home. The sun had long since fallen behind the horizon. A dark and lonely place awaited her when she opened the door to her room, but she couldn't find the strength to turn on the light. She just plopped down atop her bed, befuddled and bemused, dumbfounded and depressed; and there she lay, wide awake, all through the night, silently thinking and puzzling. But when the morning dawned, she had worked out no answer to the riddle that confounded her. It was no use; even an entire night had proved insufficient. So, giving in at last to the hunger of the morning, she rolled into a seated position and readied her numbed body for a trek to the kitchen. As the blood circulated, she gazed through her window to watch the sunrise. It was a fractured dawn, for the morning light streamed through a shattered pane; and on the sill below she beheld, on her side, a trail of uneaten seeds, and, on the other side, the cold body of a dead bluebird lying in a heap of fine glass dust.

Chapter 4

Fury

She was nearly out of ideas. **For** several days she had stalked the hallways in search of Adam, hurling hexes at him whenever he rounded a corner; but not one had had even the slightest effect on him—heck, not a single dreamy hair on his stupid head had been upset by the breeze from a swishing hand or the vehement breath blowing behind a spell!

She'd tried Magic wands—useless twigs!

She'd tried incantations—impotent lullabies!

She'd tried crystal balls—defective tenpin instruments!

She'd tried tea leaves—pathetic kitchen herbs!

She'd tried cards—*royal* waste of time!

She'd tried it all! (Or, so she would have declared, had you asked her). Nothing, absolutely *NOTHING*, was working! And now the school year was drawing to a close. Soon, Adam would be off on some kind of wonderful summer escapade, and she'd be stuck *HERE*, doing nothing more than *not* being with him!

In a rage, she began gathering up all the Magical instruments and paraphernalia she had "borrowed" from Enderbrine's, and began hurling them into the trash—and by *trash* I mean the street in front of her house.

Wands were snapped, incantation books ripped, crystal balls shattered, tea leaves danced away into the brush, and cards were taken by the wind. And then, after hurling her pocket cauldron into the street, along with any other bootless junk, she descended the stairs to the cellar, where she drew a deep breath and bent to lift the industrial-sized cauldron, that it, too, might join the rest of the rubbish. A million beads of sweat and about two near-hernias later, she gave up any hope of walking the wrecking-ball-like cauldron up the stairs.

Legs wide and fully extended before her, with her back rest-ing against the giant, curved, black body of the metal kettle, she sat there in the heart of her house, laughing mirthlessly to herself that of all the Magical trinkets she'd tried, the cauldron had been the most effective; yet, she knew no brew that would make it levitate, or sprout legs that it might evict itself, or fill her body with the strength of a hundred grizzly bears that it might be taken under her arms with ease. Such tricks might have been taught at Enderbrine's, but who could tell? Certainly not one whose study throughout every class had been the every angelic feature on Adam's dumb face—no, her studies had been far more specialized; and now, it seemed, it had all been for naught.

Still, the stories of old, in which folk found happily ever after with a one and only—those had to have been rooted in something more than just pure imagination, hadn't they? Sure, perhaps the stories *were* nothing more than dreams; but there must have been a reference point of some sort.

There must have been.

There *has* to be.

How can someone be made to want something that is one hundred percent, without a doubt, no question, hands down a fantasy?

This desire burning within her: 'twas purely natural.

And, being that nature was Magic (she was sure she'd heard that somewhere), the desire had also to be Magic; thus, through Magic could it be affected.

But how?

She had tried *everything*, hadn't she?

What else was there to—?

Just then, her eyes caught sight of a small book resting on a nearby shelf.

Sweeping slowly her legs behind her, she leaned forward onto her hands and knees, and crawled across the filthy, cluttered floor to where it sat: upon a shelf all its own, there at the bottom, untaken, to her astonishment, by the cobwebs, dust, and grime that had consumed those on the shelves above.

It was a black book; its size made its weight a surprise to the hand. And she could not tell just how many pages were contained within; for whilst giving the collection a rapid flipping, she seemed never to be able to start at the beginning, nor find the end. Though she knew she had never gazed directly at this book, or read carefully its pages, she could not help but feel that she had always known it was in her collection, and that here was the precise location in which it had always been kept; she felt, too, that she was intimate with the contents of each and every endless page. The cover demonstrated a great deal of use and handling: violent, mad handling; yet, it was more than just intact: it was also immaculate, as if tenderly tended by soft and skilled hands, on the minute, every minute. Of the pages, the same could have been said, and then some: they were solid, sturdy, stainless, and smooth; yet, each bore desperate, savage scribblings, filling every page from top to bottom, left to right, and every crack and crevice in between, rendering their respective canvases brittle, unstable, marred, and coarse. They were wild, yet calculated, the etchings; plain, but twisted; simple in fact, yet complex and not exactly complementary, cohesive, conclusive, or even coherent in explanation. They were beautiful and terrible to behold. Items bound within were listed very neatly at the start of each chapter, with expert penmanship and careful crafting. How delightful to the eye were these items, and all the more wonderful for the heart to speak! Sketches made of delicately crafted lines and shapes spotted the pages here and there; and all around the focal item, inked in the very center of the page, were the words used to describe, explain, and capture the encircled. How gracefully they began, these words, wrapping easily the source of their life; but as the circle grew, some of the letters forming those words began to bend and twist, to forget its way along the path of its formation, soon warping entire words, crumpling clauses, stretching and shattering sentences, and paralyzing paragraphs, until a chaotic whirlwind rushed through pages upon pages of unbounded, relentless grammatical cacophonies.

Adeline poured over these, fascinated, elated, transfixed, and terrified, flipping through page after page, reading nothing and knowing all, whilst bursts and rushes of searing lightning, raging fire, and crashing waves flooded her chest. And she did this for some time, until her heart began to pound with such piercing pain that she collapsed, prostrate before the book, in a puddle of cold sweat.

Her breath did not soon return.

When finally it did, she lifted her eyes to the text lying open before her.

How much deeper might run the rivers of such a text, she wondered?

Adeline lay before the book with trembling.

Perhaps, thought she, this collection might be better read upstairs in her room, the place in which she did much of her thinking, where things could be made clear; not like here, in this cold, dusty, and dingy old cellar.

But when she moved to lift the book from the shelf, she found it could not be budged. A quick examination revealed the culprit: a mighty, metal link bound to the base of the book's spine and falling into the base of the bookshelf, where it was surely and securely fastened to something she could not see.

How curious, thought she—here, bound in the depths; yet, familiar. But how ever might it be known if read here? If it could not be lifted to her room to be studied in the proper environment, how ever was she to fully understand?

The thought of tearing the pages and taking them with her did indeed cross her mind and flow into her fingers; but of this she was made mortally afraid. For when she began carefully to tear the first page, its body began to burst into a mist, and she knew any further tearing might surely cause it to disintegrate entirely. An oddly satisfying, relieving experience; yet, one her heart did regard with dread. And, so, without another option coming to mind, she settled in before the opened book and took to a detailed reading of the contents therein.

Hours passed, and deeper she fell into the spiraling words, feeling their desperation, their ardent desire to burst forth—so acute was the essence of each word, bound beneath the sounds, syllables, sentences, and the ink used to compose them, like a rabid bull wrapped in a *papier mâché* straightjacket; she knew their meaning as a razor through her flesh; yet, though it seemed such could not have been possible, she failed to understand both the individual entries and the book in which they were bound.

Onward, still, she read; and as she did so, the book's pages became heavier, denser; each met the touch of her fingers with a sensation of deep saturation. And in the air there hung a great cloud of invisible fumes, rising from the ink as it bled over her skin and seeped through her eyes.

Deeper and deeper still; the pages were like mighty leather straps, coiling about her heart, tightening, squeezing, making it pound and rattle painfully; until, at long last, when her eyes had been so blackened by the pouring ink and her mind overflowing with the intoxicating drink leaking from the barbs of every spiraling word, she knew at last the cry lifting from the pages, its lament, its desperation: Emptiness.

How the walls of her heart ached with every pound, like bare flesh against stone—'twas the cold, hard, brutal, and jagged boulder of reality that beat against the tenderness of her heart, a reality that screamed of a void, this emptiness, growing like a cancer deep within: an unjust emptiness, forged by all she had been denied, all that Magic had failed her heart to realize… until now.

Her eyes raining streams of black, she rose from the floor; and with her blackened hands rising to the heavens, she called and cast forth a Magic rare in the light of the sun, yet endemic within and revealed by the shadows as the birthright of all: the Curse.

Every piercing, spiraling word, their epicenters, every page, and the all-consuming ink that flowed from it all: these led ever and only to one conclusion, one method, one type of Magic that would surely erupt like a geyser every drop that had from hand to page been penned, and thereafter form into a mighty river all that had been trapped within, flowing, raging against the emptiness that pervaded her weary heart, filling it at last with every desperate desire long denied—one method: a Curse, to shake the foundations of all that had once obstructed the way to real, Magical salvation!

Her head falling back, she parted wide her lips; and as her eyes beheld in the darkness that which was made crystal clear by the eruptions breaking against the now fortified walls of her once weak and tender heart, she spoke the words that were of a heart churning now violently like a lake of fire coursing deep within:

"Waves of flame! Arise! Arise!
"And scorch his Earth, melt his Skies!
"Now, to see his World undone,
"To bring an ever setting sun!

"Undo Beauty! Mar his face!
"Nest a stiffness in his grace!
"Torment his flesh! Break and twist!
"Open wounds! Let sickness persist!

"Destroy his wealth! Raze his home!
"Eat his robes and let him roam
"A naked, noisome, vile beast
"To crawl and moan, and on dirt feast!
"Harvest then a heart reborn, else be this his eternal thorn!"

So great was the power that burst forth from the depths of her heart that she fell limp and lifeless, as one dead, into a heap on the floor. And there, lying with her face turned upward, she watched through sealed eyes her Curse take hold and ravage the one by whom she had ever wished to know that which she'd hoped was Love, until, as a tear fell slowly along the side of her face and into her ear, there was stillness, followed by slits of white light running over her eyes, and a throbbing pain in her forehead.

Chapter 5
Chemistry

Another year at Enderbrine's had come to an end. It mattered not, however, how many years remained until traditional completion; this would be the last year.

There were no exit papers, no formal renunciation, no instructors standing at the door, begging for reconsideration, nor was there any word or hint of terminus spoken or given to anyone on that final day within the halls of Enderbrine's; for that day became the last day the day before the first day of the next year (or, for those of us who haven't yet had our morning coffee, the decision to not return to Enderbrine's occurred the day preceding the start of the new semester).

It was not uncommon for students to throw their generously-labeled "education" by the wayside when some other shiny obsession captured the interest, or the shininess that had drawn them to a previous interest (like Enderbrine's) had inevitably faded. Rarely had it anything to do with the will of a parent, for what student heeded the impotent Magic of Parenting anyway?

Throughout the summer, not a single second of consideration had been given to *not* returning; little thought had been given to Enderbrine's at all, in fact; and that which had been given foresaw a return as a certainty requiring no further attention. But something happened that summer—many things happened, actually; so many things rolled up into one giant mess that when it came time once again to reenter the Magical halls, more than just (as Enderbrine's would have defined it) the Magic of Shame stood in the way.

It all began with an interrupting *knock*.

"You Adam?"

"*You* know what time it is?" said the groggy, grumpy, and bedheaded youth, rubbing his eyes and casting a scowl at the unwelcome annoyance perched upon his doorstep, fouling up his start of the summer holiday.

"Funny. Sign here."

"What? Why? What is this? Who are you?"

"I represent the bank."

"The *who*?"

"The people who own this place—and the people who, furthermore, have had no reply to the many letters sent regarding this very document. Sign here."

"What are you talking—? Oh, go away. I'm going back to bed."

"You feel free to do so," the voice replied, as a hand stopped the door Adam had just given a peeved swing, "provided you first sign here, and that your bed is moved to at least over there."

Speaking thusly, the self-identified bank representative pointed to a patch of overgrown earth just beyond the property.

"Excuse *me*?" returned Adam, his eyes widening with rage at the idiotic suggestion and relentless intrusion on his vacation and slumber.

"The bank is evicting you. Sign here to approve this," said the man, extending an arm to a moving truck parked in the driveway: "an undeserved courtesy, compliments of the bank."

"Wait, wait, wait…you'd better be *giving* me that truck! Are you suggesting I *move*, or something?"

"Not suggesting. Ordering. And not on my own or authority, nor the bank's."

With this, the man handed Adam a legal document, spelling out in painfully thorough detail just how much Adam no longer lived in his castle.

"But…how?"

"Nothing is free. And when you neglect to pay for the thing daddy gives you, well…we did send letters, you know."

Adam's face had been drained of all color; his eyes were locked in a dead, dumbfounded stare, falling heavily onto the face of the man before him, and broken only when there came a great rumbling, which soon materialized into a massive piece of machinery, boasting a towering arm, to which was attached a giant wrecking ball.

The bank representative, who had not turned to regard the demolition machine, loudly tapped his clipboard to recapture Adam's attention.

"You'll want to be signing here."

***

"Since *when?* Two nights I've had to sleep in that stupid truck waiting to get in here and set you *idiots* straight!"

"Your frustration is understandable, sir; however, our hours *are* clearly stated, available through several mediums, and have been consistent since our opening more than one hundred years ago."

"Whatever! I want to know why I haven't been able to withdraw any of my money!"

"All of your accounts have been depleted. Have you not been receiving the notices we've been sending?"

"And why aren't any of my cards working? I tried to buy

food two nights ago, and all of my cards were declined! What the heck are you people even *doing* over here?"

"Sir, I'm very sorry, but you've racked up so much debt. This has become a rather grave legal matter."

"What do you mean *debt*? No, no, no; do you have any idea how much money my fath—I mean, there's no way *all* that money is gone!"

"Your assets have been seized in order to pay your debts. The bank has already auctioned its repossessed property to balance our end. Amazingly, you come out of all this owing only the bank, and very little at that."

"I don't owe you a darned thing! YOU owe ME! YOU *stole* my house—demolished it! YOU stole my money! YOU are the ones who owe!"

"Sir, in light of the extreme circumstances, the bank is willing to consider forgiving the remaining amount, if—"

"I don't care! I am so beyond DONE with you people! Just shut up and give me back my stuff!"

"I'm afraid that's not possible, sir."

"NOW!"

"Sir, I'm trying to explain that—"

CRASH

"Please, sir! If you don't calm—"

SMASH

"Someone call security!"

"SHUT UP! SHUT UP! JUST SHUT UP!"

***

He had never known cold like this. Not even his rage could

warm him as he lay there in the moonlight streaming through the steel bars on the outer wall of his cage.

If there was an upside to this new situation, it was that he'd had his first meal in two days, served shortly after arriving. He'd gotten off easy; or, so he'd been told: no charges were being pressed by the bank, leaving him to pay only a minimum sentence for his conduct with those who'd carried him away—this he did by forfeiting the contents of the moving truck, leaving him with only the clothes on his back, legs, and feet.

From behind the elevated desk, and before the sound of the mallet that would order him caged for seven days, he'd been informed that he would be forever barred from the bank, unable to enter the building or reopen his now permanently closed accounts; but he was also informed that his debt had, even after his destructive outburst, been forgiven. He who had spoken these words seemed not to like the way those last few had tasted upon his tongue. Adam was then escorted to his new dwelling, where his only possessions were exchanged for the standard uniform sported by the inhabitants of this enclosure of cages, before being placed into storage.

It would be a long seven days, watching the summer world go by without him, being served poor excuses for food, having nothing but a growing body odor and the pungent stench from the tin can in the corner to keep him company.

There was nothing to do, except think.

Adam was not exactly known for his thinking.

Still, he reasoned, better to get lost in the head than to experience the weight of reality.

And so he did.

Day One of his stay overflowed with rage-filled thinking. There seemed not enough hours in the day to name all those who had been at fault in the present ruining of his life! If the hasty summer sun would only slow its darned horses, he might have been able to avoid the heavy eyes of the evening and add a couple more names to his list of "People I Will NEVER Forgive," or, perhaps it was better entitled "Sweet Revenge." By the time he'd fallen asleep, he hadn't yet decided which of the two titles he liked better, or if he might combine them—something like, "Sweet Revenge on the People I Will NEVER Forgive." Something like that.

And so ended Day One, with a horizon blackened by the absence of a sun long since asleep, and three plates of food and glasses of water sitting untouched by the cage door.

Day Two was, in many ways, similar to Day One. Off to a slow start, Day Two began several hours after the sun had breached the horizon. His eyes fluttering open, he turned to see one plate of food and a glass of water at the door, as well as an incredibly large man holding another of the same. Saying nothing, the man opened the door and set the plate and glass inside, before turning without a word to push a cart filled with more plates and glasses to be delivered to neighboring cages. But Adam, though he had yet the strength to stand—or, at the very least, fall to the floor and crawl—would not budge. He stared at the plate, his mouth watering, his stomach gurgling, and his muscles quaking. But he would not rise. Instead, he slowly sealed his eyes and drifted into a dream, in which the names on the mental list he'd made appeared scrawled upon an aged piece of parchment. And as the ink that formed each name melted into tiny balls that rolled to his colossal feet, he gazed from wide and hungry eyes, hung over the page like aviation lights on a skyscraper, as the blobs sprouted into the forms of the people behind the etchings. With a maniacal laugh, he gleefully lifted his gigantic foot, casting an all-consuming shadow over the people. And as their shrieks of terror and pleas for mercy filled the void, mixing with his laughter, a force unlike any he had ever known, took hold of his nape and dragged him through the darkness, at what must have been fifty times the speed of light, to a quickly approaching white hole.

Day Three began with a jolt, and the words, "Boss says you gotta eat somethin' today;" after which his mouth was stuffed full with a gooey, tasteless slop.

Spitting it out with a retch, Adam rolled off the concrete bed and began to scamper away from whatever it was that had forced the stuff into his mouth. But his efforts were not only futile, they were also and moreover counterproductive; for the more he struggled, the weaker he became, until he was at last more ragdoll than man, unable even to move his own jaw.

Lazy eyes rolled about the room before finally steadying and focusing their gaze on a bear of a man sitting beside him on the floor with his back against the concrete bed, holding a bowl of something in one hand, and carefully working Adam's jaw with the other.

"I can't make you swallow," (though, it sounded more like *swalla*), "but you'll be rid of me a lot sooner if you do."

Still, Adam resisted. If *swalla*-ing was the only thing over which he had control, then, by golly, he was going to exercise that control until he got his way or died.

The slop, now more liquefied, leaked through his weary lips.

The bear caught it in the bowl.

With a heavy sigh (and a tiny chuckle), the bear-man said, "Well, ain't you a stubborn little stoat! But I've got all day." The word "day" came with a giggle; Adam's blood boiled. "And, like it or not, or throw it up later, I'm gettin' somethin' in that tummy—no matter how long it takes."

It would take quite a while.

The bear sat there with Adam all day, in fact.

And, though he fell asleep with an empty stomach, this night would be the warmest of his stay.

When he awoke on Day Four, Adam found the bear still sitting beside him. A temporary clarity filled his head, and he realized that he had spent all of the previous day cradled in a giant's embrace; not only that, he had also in that embrace had a most memorable slumber, unsullied (despite his best efforts) even by the fact that his pillow had been an enormous, squishy belly.

Looking up, he beheld a set of huge eyes, gazing back at him, *swalla*-ing him; they bore a sort of "What's it gonna be, today?" kind of look.

Adam shot bolt upright.

Doing so, however, transferred his sluggish, nutrient-deprived blood clean out of his brain; and he collapsed like a dead fish into the rippling waterbed that was the bear's belly.

"Whadda ya say?" asked the voice attached to the belly, heard as an earthquake, rumbling muted yet mighty; it filled his ears as water from a broken dam and rattled his brain into focus.

When his head was lifted by a power not his own, Adam tossed about in his sluggish brain a few smart, stinging remarks to hurl in protest of his treatment thus far. However, even if anything coherent could have been formed, he had not strength enough to lift it. And, so, straining as would a powerlifter against a world record weight, Adam contorted his face into the best scowl his convulsing facial muscles could manage; and, in his mind, he added the name Bear to his yet untitled list.

Heaving a heavy sigh, Bear lifted Adam clean off the floor and carried him to his concrete bed, where he deposited the weary lad before exiting the cage.

"At last!" declared Adam somewhere within his brain (wherever *that* was at present), and then gazed out through the steel bars that filled a small opening at the top of the outer wall of his cage, there to curse the sun as it bestowed summertime fun on everyone but him.

And there he stayed for quite some time, boiling with a fiery rage that would have given all of Earth's nearest stars combined a run for their money; until he had become so violently wrathful against the daylight that he gazed directly into the sun's blinding body, as if to intimidate it into a swift retreat, or blast it with such a vicious glare that it was knocked into another universe.

To his astonishment, it would not take long for the sun's power to dim. Indeed, not five seconds into his plan to intimidate or stare-punch the sun, those gleaming, daytime rays were erased, the glowing fire burning about the star's body was extinguished, and the perfect sphere that remained was beset with shadow, one so great that the entire world was made all the darker.

"Seen many a masochist in my day," came a booming voice from somewhere to his left; and when Adam looked, he saw naught but pitch black with a fuzzy greenish-orange dot floating about his center of vision; "and I would say that you take the cake—I would indeed, if, of course, you'd stoop to actually taking a cake."

Adam would certainly have been grinding his teeth at the sound of that most aggravating chuckle following the voice, had not his attention been stolen by Bear's having tapped with one of his sausage fingers directly on top of Adam's left eye, only to be stopped by a shield of darkened plastic. When a startled Adam whipped his hands to his face, he peeled away a set of sunglasses. Instantly, the room burst into light.

Squinting as a cave dweller emerging for the first time into the great wide-open, Adam was quickly made aware of another sensation: his feet were being attacked by an octopus! Casting his twitching eyes downward, he beheld Bear's giant figure, holding a towel and kneeling before a bowl, where, having removed Adam's shoes and socks, he had begun to wash his feet.

"Usually where the stink starts, right here," said Bear, his eyes fixed upon his task.

Adam, repulsed but unable to retaliate, watched helplessly, while tormenting waves of embarrassment and disgust coursed through him. And these things he fought tooth and nail to maintain, even as his feet announced that there had never been a set of hands quite so tender and understanding as Bear's, or when the stale, yellowish cloud that had been growing and hovering just below nostril-level began to dissipate—or when his nose mistook his toeses for roses.

"There!" declared Bear.

And as he exited the room, he nodded his head toward the side of Adam's concrete bed, where sat a pile of laundered clothes, as well as plate of hot, freshly-baked cookies next to a tall glass of ice-cold milk.

Day Five looked like rain. The clouds were heavy and low, but one drop only did the concrete know this day.

Rolling onto his side, Adam regarded the pile of dusty clothes, as well as the now stale cookies and curdled milk. And as he did so, his mind was taken to a subject on which it had worked consciously and daily not to dwell for years: his father.

He knew such wastefulness would displease the old man, should he be here to see it. And, no doubt, there would be a word or two (at the *very* least) about the present situation. Adam greatly disliked the subject of his father; even discussions or mentions of others' fathers, or fathers in general, were enough to push his buttons, particularly those labeled with the word (or synonyms of) "Irritate."

No fond memory lay at the end of any cord running from the subject his mind would presently not release from its focus. Oh, how the man would preach! Adam was never starved for an opinion from the old man, that's for sure. Minutes felt like days whenever unavoidable, often father-manufactured, circumstances had joined their paths, like all those times his father would insist on accompanying him to the gas station—the gas station! What, did he not think his son was capable of pumping his own gas without supervision? Ridiculous! But, most revolting of all, was how his father would look at him: eyebrows like two feathers falling through a calm desert; eyes that looked like they'd just been painted with a glossy glaze; great big bags under those eyes; wrinkles all pulled toward his nose; and lips pinched tightly together, pressing inward against his teeth—what a pathetic, infuriating look of disappointment and disapproval.

As that face grew sharper in his mind, Adam was taken back to the last time he'd seen it, a day that was also the last time he'd seen his father. The old man said very little that day, but that look of his was as potent as ever it had been. With a huff, Adam had snatched from his father's hand the keys to his new house, and then turned away, happy to never again see the face behind the voice that, in that moment, mumbled something he couldn't have cared less to hear, before leaving in whatever way its bearer had seen fit.

Adam had neither the strength nor the inclination to replay those mumbled tones in his head until they formed a coherent mixture of communicative sound, but there was one particular collection of sound that swirled about his mind like a giant fish in a tiny bowl: his own voice, speaking what would be his last words to his father: "Just give me what is mine."

He had never regretted those words; even now it could not have been said that his heart felt anything near to contrition. However, he did wonder if, perhaps...well, it's hard to say, really. For what name can be given to a foreign sensation, if the one experiencing it has naught but his own history from which to draw and identify it? This tiny twist in his gut, one so much different than the burning hunger to which he was becoming rather accustomed...can thought breed feeling?

There would be no more thinking on this matter, for at that

moment Bear entered the cage, pushing his cart, lined, as usual, with meals for the block. As he had many times, Bear, looking down at a wasting Adam, lying now on his hollow belly, with one arm dangling over his concrete slab, heaved a heavy sigh; and, saying not a word, he lifted the stale cookies and curdled milk from Adam's stagnant field of vision.

Adam waited, staring now at an empty patch of floor, for the usual slop, or a penalizing serving of nothing, to fall before him.

And then, to his astonishment, his nose was greeted by the intoxicating, salivation-inducing, tummy-teasing aroma of freshly baked cookies, which soon grew so strong it formed into a plate stacked high—twice as high as the previous plate—with the most beautiful, cooked-to-perfection delights his eyes had ever beheld; and, right beside them, was placed a glass of milk, ever so tall and dripping with tell of cool refreshment.

Bear said nothing.

Adam listened as the wobbly wheels of the meal cart exited his cage.

And to the concrete did fall a single drop of rain.

Adam slept not a wink that night. And on the morning of Day Six, after hours upon hours, lying on his backside, cursing and reviling every urge and viciously wrestling every feeling beckoning the rain to fall, a small clearing of the throat snapped his attention to his cage's door, beside which, on a folding chair, sat Bear.

Adam had had enough of these games.

Digging deep, he summoned a violent rage, roaring fires and tempestuous winds—enough to lift his wasted frame to his feet.

And as the room began to twirl and spin, Adam stooped to the floor, took up the plate of now stale cookies and curdled milk, and hurled them with all his might at Bear.

The glass of milk shattered against the giant man's face; he was made absolutely drenched. Soon after, the plate broke upon his chest; the cookies thereon exploded into a fine dust that stuck to the milk on Bear's face and clothes, making a sort of paste that oozed alongside the curdled chunks.

When the tumult of breaking glass and shattering ceramic had at last ceased, Adam looked up from the floor to which his over-exerted legs had dropped his bag of bones; and there he beheld Bear, sitting yet as he had before the attack, unmoved, with gobs of wet cookie falling from his body, and a mixture of white and red raining down his face.

The pair sat for a few moments without speaking, locked in the other's stare. And then, still saying nothing, Bear rose, extracted a handkerchief to clean his hands, and then scooped Adam from the floor before depositing him onto the concrete slab.

Incensed, Adam lifted his hand to strike Bear across the face; but his fist was stayed when his partially blurred vision, made clear by the proximity, caught sight of a shard of glass imbedded deeply into Bear's cheek, just below the eye; blood leaked from the wound as water through a cracked dam. And, bombarded with rushes of mental and emotional confusion and conflict—like a screaming avalanche and the seething fury of a violent volcano's pyroclastic flow colliding upon a single point that was his very being—Adam fell into a state of dark oblivion, whence he would not emerge for some time.

There, in the void, Adam wandered.

For a great, long while, naught but blackness swaddled him. And through this nothingness, he drifted; until, at last, there appeared a faint light, flickering in the distance—whether dying or growing, he cold not readily tell; whether emerging or retreating could not be immediately discerned. Long, indeed, did he ponder the flame.

Spans of indeterminate time seemed to be passing; he had to take some sort of action. He did not walk toward it; though, his legs moved as if to do so. It was obvious to him that he was not covering any ground; the imperceptible surface beneath him passed under his feet like the belt of a treadmill. Rather, the light approached him; or, perhaps, it grew in size, becoming bigger and bigger, until its body had become so massive that its expanding walls swallowed him whole.

There inside the flame, Adam perceived not the heart of fire, but rather the home of his father. And there before him stood the patriarch himself, appearing as one who had stepped forth from an aged photograph: a boy, tinted a shade of amber, and not exactly clear in feature. His clothes matched those one might have expected to see from the youth of days past; only, these robes were well-used, quite beyond their appointed time of retirement. And, yet, upon the boy's face was a look of boundless happiness.

As the flame grew larger, the boy drew nearer to Adam and became older in age, while the walls of the expanding flame, which carried in their blazing form the very features of the house surrounding the boy, were simultaneously changed, becoming more than the rotting, crudely crafted, and poorly placed wood they had been. Why Adam had not noticed at first that the walls of his father's house were so derelict he could not say. Perhaps it had been because they were too common or unimpressive to be of note in this bizarre journey through the void. Or, perhaps it had something to do with seeing his father as a boy. Maybe, even, it had had something to do with the boy's smile, one just as unaware of its surroundings as Adam had in looking at it been rendered.

These new walls were walls fit for a king compared to the ones left behind; still, they were nowhere in the vicinity of his standard for passable, much less perfect. Amid them, standing nearer now to Adam, was his father, looking near to Adam's age; the amber tint had nearly fallen away completely, and much of the blurriness had been sharpened. His hands were noticeably beaten: great callouses coated his fingers and palms; gashes and scabs, and some open wounds, were painted in grisly colors. They were broken, yet strong, these hands; and about one tattered finger had been woven a ring of gold. The young man had acquired new clothes, but even these appeared in great need of replacing. And upon his dirty face was worn a smile, one—if it could be believed, given all there was to see—so much grander and brighter than the one worn by the boy of a mere moment past.

Again the flame grew, and again his father was brought nearer, now into almost perfect clarity. He was, at this stage, very much as Adam had always remembered him, with only wrinkles and greys missing from the presentation. Standing in the grand halls Adam recalled from his youth, adorned with great wealth and riches, glittering like diamonds and jewels, his father wore a blue, tailored suit with golden cufflinks. Not one hair upon his head was out of place; not one patch of fabric knew a wrinkle; and, quite beyond belief, not a single bit of light or rapture had been lost from his smile—it was, in fact, as grand as ever it had been. This was a man who, if that smile grew any further, might explode into light itself.

While his father's posture had been consistent throughout the first two movements, facing forward with his hands at his sides, he stood now with his smiling face pointed toward his left arm, bent, with his left hand touching the center of his chest— 'twas like a tender cradling of the air.

Adam stood puzzling for what seemed like a long while, scanning every detail of the stagnant image. But then, very slowly, the smile on his father's face began to fail, and about his eyes there pooled tears. In that same moment, the walls of the flame began to contract, pulling Adam's father, still cradling the air, away into the distance. The house walls—which had been so luxurious and grand, which had glittered like diamonds and jewels—were beset with fog, muted, as if painted lightly with a stroke of grey. His father was not spared this greying; though, his image became ever clearer as he drifted away: his hair began to lose its color and his face was gradually marred by age.

The flame continued to collapse, taking his father deeper and deeper into the distance; yet, with the increase in distance, his father's image was made paradoxically stark.

Further and further he went, until Adam stood with his back against the wall of flame. What diamonds and jewels had hung upon the grand walls had been stolen by the now deepening darkness; and Adam, feeling the frigid cold of the outside ca-ressing his spine, saw in clarity, far exceeding the eye of a hawk peering through a telescope, his father's face: that glowing smile now erased, replaced with a mien of inconsolable grief that was washed bitterly by a storm of tears raining from above.

At last, the flame retreated, leaving Adam behind. As its glow faded into the distance, a great chill began to grow; and grow it did, hastily, until the flame was gone, at which point the void became a whirlwind of unbearable cold. But Adam suffered not long enough to feel his skin quake and shiver, for out from within the darkness there came a great force to block the wind. A reddish glow was painted over his eyes, but he could not see clearly; and it was then that he realized his eyes were closed. But, given the power of the glow seen through veiled eyes, Adam dared not unseal them. Rather, he waited, trembling, though not by the icy hand that surrounded him—something mighty and bright stood before him; he could sense its magnificent presence, hear the wind rustling against it to no avail, while beneath the howl there boomed the sound and sensation of warm and steady breathing.

A mere moment later, this great presence fell upon him, wrapping him from head to toe in warmth like he'd never known; and against every urge to fall helplessly into the grand power encircling him and slumber unto eternity, Adam opened his eyes with a flutter.

It was Day Seven.

Through the steel bars high above him blew a frigid wind. But it could not touch him, for about him had been wrapped a giant blanket, and beneath him had been placed a mattress.

And from the foot of the bed, having just tucked the blanket under Adam's feet, emerged Bear, who then drifted through the daytime night to the cage door.

***

"Wake up!

"Hey! C'mon—let's go!

"Wake up! It's time.

"Somebody get this punk outta here!"

Day Eight: Freedom.

After being awakened by a most unfriendly-looking face rattling a nightstick in the cage bars, Bear was called down to Adam's cage to prepare him for discharge. Seven long days of confinement had at last come to an end. But this was presently neither here nor there for Adam; his mind and body were far too weak to really process anything at all.

Like a ragdoll in Bear's mighty arms, Adam was jostled about for what seemed like quite a while, before being lifted and dragged into the main office, where at last his blood discovered his feet and performed the basic function of standing. He felt a bit heavier, Adam, as if his torso were a bloated skyscraper balancing on a pair of toothpicks; but all of his vital systems seemed out of whack; so, of what note was this sensation among the dense and obnoxious cast of others, such as the feeling of pencil tips trying to puncture his skin from within, or the party of translucent bubbles dancing about his eyes?

Words were tossed about in the dim and stuffy space; they mixed with a droning hum that Adam could not and cared not to identify. Eventually, after a great deal of waiting and swaying like a buoy in a mildly miffed sea, a piece of paper was pushed before him and a pen was fitted into his limp hand.

Whatever that limp hand had produced was deemed sufficient to satisfy the requirement of "signature."

Shortly thereafter, Adam, wearing now the clothes he'd donned when entering this place, found himself standing before a large, metal door; and when it was opened, a glorious morning—bright and warm, filled with the songs of birds, the fresh smells of newness matured, and a rush of sunshine that seemed to melt the weak-and-weariness, as if it had been a block of ice encasing him—raced forth and snatched him from the gloom of confinement. Still, alive and strong though he felt, his physical state remained as one whose bed lies six feet below Earth's green face. And, so, to get his legs used once again to the rhythm of their purpose, Bear walked with Adam one mile.

"That's it," said Bear, pointing ahead. "Up there is where I leave you. When we get there, you keep on walkin'. And don't you stop!" he commanded, dropping a sausage finger into the panting chest leaning against his body. "You carry this to the end, you hear? There'll be a lot of places to stop and lie down along the way; they'll be dressed with signs tellin' you they got what you need—tellin' you what paths to take, too. But you just keep on walkin'!"

About to be on his own again in a world in which he bore nothing to his name, save for the clothes on his back and the weight pressing against his heels, Adam's brain divorced itself from the stubbornness of the thumping organ just below, which had set itself firmly upon never speaking to or looking upon Bear; and, switching to autopilot, the same brain not only ordered the eyes to look at Bear squarely in the face, but also mobilized the tongue to speak.

"How will I know which paths to take? Where, even, am I going?"

"Here," said Bear, dropping a backpack onto Adam's shoulders; and, giving the pack a heavy, hearty pat that prematurely expelled Adam's next breath, he added, "Your map. As for where you're goin'…well, I'd say that's up to you, now."

All at once, Bear's feet came to a halt; and with a shove he sent Adam on his way.

"Keep walkin'!" he called into our co-titular-character's wake. "And don't you look back, to the left, or to the right! Eyes ahead! The map is yours now, as is the choice!"

After a great deal of walking, Adam's feet ached so badly that he could practically hear them pleading a simple (yet, very detailed) and rather convincing case for him to halt. But Bear's words would not leave his mind, despite his best efforts. And, so, Adam reasoned that perhaps he could lighten the load on his feet and ease their suffering. Surely, thought he, the backpack could be tossed. While not exactly sure of a point, purpose, or direction, Adam was confident he knew this part of the world well enough to get him to a place of comfort and security—so, of what use was Bear's map? Reasoning thusly, he lifted the backpack to cast it to the side of the road; but as he did so, he found that it bore no weight at all. It was so light, he noted, that it might just float to the clouds should he release it. But what, then, thought he, was causing this weight he'd begun to feel just before departing? His bodyweight was lighter than ever, and this particular pain was not due to a strain on weak muscles. No, this was something entirely different. And, examining himself, Adam determined that his clothes must have been the culprits—that is, what foreign objects he soon identified bulging from their pockets. Digging into them, Adam discovered in his back two pockets and his right hip pocket three bottles of water, one stuffed in each; and in his left hip pocket, he found a protein-packed energy snack bar. His hunger and thirst immediately erupted into wild, maniacal whoops of joy and screams of desperation; so great were these eruptions, he nearly lost his feet. Quickly scanning the area, Adam saw that there was no one around—naught but the trees along the dirt road could behold his actions. Such was good enough for him; and, before his next breath, Adam had banished the cap of a water bottle, shredded the snack bar's wrapper, and commenced a feral inhaling of both. All the world seemed to fade into empty light as his teeth sunk through the soft, chocolaty tissue of the bar, his slaver washing its delectable flavor over his tongue, touching each and every bud as would the live end of a power cable; his saliva bubbled and boiled, mixing the sweet, salty, and savory juices into a heavenly brew; his tongue was like a sponge, absorbing rivers of ecstasy into its every fiber, before releasing a tsunami of pleasure back into his mouth to be swished and swashed, just to rapturously suck it back up again; every gulp of water was like a summer rain falling over his face and a mighty waterfall flooding his entire body; its coolness banished the heat from his weary flesh as steam from sun-beaten asphalt, while paradoxically sending raging streams of fire through his muscles and into his head, calling forth sweat from his brow; oh, how delightful and distinguished was its taste, so stark against the flavor bleeding about his teeth; 'twas like drinking a winter wind, lapping a cloud, or sipping the moments separating the day from the night. And as these enrapturing sensations overtook him, Adam could have sworn he heard over the stillness of the air a familiar chuckle, one that had once caused his blood to boil, but was now, in spite of himself, a sort of pleasantly chaotic music, like the tinkling tune of a wind chime, happily caught in the breath of a playful springtime breeze.

***

At daybreak, it dawned on Adam that he had walked all through the night.

Ahead, he perceived the path on which he and Bear had embarked the morning prior; it was narrowing, though it showed no signs of being consumed by the Earth: weeds grew in abundance along its edges, but they could not penetrate the rich soil that was the path; theirs was a razor-straight line along its edges. The further his feet trod along the narrowing way, the slower his pace became—soon, he reasoned, he would reach an unknown end in a wood he knew not.

Where, then, would he be?

About the time this thought (and a hundred more like it) had reached a crescendo in his head, like a set of giant cymbals boxing his ears, he saw to his left—just beyond the weeds, and surrounded by a beautiful ring of smooth stones—a wide, dirt parking lot; and, set behind it all, was a most welcome sight: a hotel, one standing tall and bearing many windows and glass doors, through which burst forth dazzling colors, soothing, sensational sounds, and from which enchanting perfumes and intoxicating aromas drifted through his nose and into his heart like the scent of delicate and sure-to-be delicious delights baking in an oven.

Without a second thought, Adam diverted his feet into the weeds. Surely food and rest could be found here, he thought. What offering can blind wandering make to meet the immediate callings? So eager he must have been—or, perhaps it was that his weak legs had simply gotten used to the rhythm found in the soft earth—that the moment he stepped off the path, a force, as if he had been caught by a fishing hook and line, or yanked by a magnet, pulled him backward, dropping his rump with a merciless *THUD* into the weeds. And, what would prove even more unfortunate, when he again found his feet and proceeded toward the ring of rocks, his legs perceived an increasing weight, which only grew as he advanced toward the hotel, doubtlessly as a result of his muscles having lost the momentum of movement.

He, eventually, with no small effort, made it all the way across the dirt parking lot; and when at last he fell through the door, he was panting so hard and sweating bullets enough to supply a besieged army for a week that he could not draw breath enough to demand a room, much less see through the waterfalls raining over his eyes anyone at whom to direct his demand.

"Oh, dear!" cried a voice, manifesting beside him as if from thin air, even without so much as a warning from approaching footsteps. "Aren't *you* a weary traveler! *Dolores*! Bread and water! Quickly!"

Adam felt his head being lifted.

"Easy, son," breathed the voice; and soon there was a soft, tender sensation pressing gently against his eyes, which soon restored his sight.

"That's better."

Adam turned, and there, framed perfectly in streaming rays of bright light, falling like heavenly rain through the glass door and over a set of masculine shoulders, was a most handsome man—perhaps the finest looking man Adam had ever beheld, with strong but very elegant features that appeared to have been expertly chiseled with the sole purpose of magnifying that which was even brighter than the light pouring in through the door: the man's smile.

"The name's Lucius," he said, stuffing a sweat-soaked handkerchief into his shirt pocket and slowly lifting Adam into a seated position against the railing post of the staircase behind them. "And what might your name be?"

Taking in the experience that was beholding such a face, dressed with long, golden hair, touched only, it seemed, by what age had been specifically, selectively invited to ferry youth unto mature beauty, Adam now paused to appreciate how like a baritone choir were the notes dripping from Lucius' lips.

"Adam," our leading male returned with labored speech.

"A fine name, indeed! Tell me, Adam," said Lucius, settling down beside him and draping an arm over his shoulders, "where might these tired legs have been carrying you, eh? Not much to see down *that* road."

"What road?"

"The little dirt road, just yonder," he replied with a dismissive, flailing point through the glass door. "I was watching you."

"You were?"

"It's my business to do so! I know a weary traveler when I see one; and you, son," he cheered, pressing a finger into Adam's chest, "are a *most* weary traveler! People like you are the reason I keep glass doors and widows: to see and prepare a space for the wayward, even before they've neared my door, and also to let those same wanderers see that in my hotel are comforts and pleasures untold! Speaking of which…"

It was at this moment that a burst of light, alike in brilliance to the one Adam had seen over Lucius, was unveiled from within the wall to his right. And, standing in its midst, was a most angelic creature: a silhouette against the extraordinary, calming blue glow that was like a frame of flame wrapped tightly about this radiant being; and in Adam there arose a fire that warmed and sedated whatever tension he might yet have been feeling.

"Dolores! Come! Meet Adam. My boy," said Lucius, as the angelic figure glided toward them, "this is my daughter, Dolores."

Before his mind (which was still transfixed with the silhouette in blue standing in the opposite doorway) could catch up to the moment, Adam's eyes were wide and staring at a black-haired fantasy of beauty, a woman the likes of whom even a goddess would behold with envy; and to him—yes, to *him*—she was singing a sweet symphony that was in composition but a single, enchanting word: "Hello."

After what might very well have been an hour or two, Adam realized that perhaps it was his turn to offer a salutation. But, before any could be mustered and lifted to his lips, Lucius said with a chuckle, "I think the young man might find his tongue if it were first washed in food and drink, my dear."

A hand from the heavens reached forth and painted a soft and rather tranquilizing smile upon the fair lady's face; and, as Adam watched, trembling, she peeled back behind her ear a lock of her midnight black hair, and lifted to his lips her cup.

Her delicate, redolent fingers seemed to bear a glow about their beautiful, porcelain bodies; and when his trembling caused his mouth to dribble streams of water, her touch upon his face and accompanying, widening smile, bearing to him her perfect, radiant teeth, nearly hurled him into a swoon.

Like a rush of all-consuming fire, the food and drink Adam had been given made him feel more awake and alive than he had in quite some time, perhaps ever; and as it digested, a regard, building toward something far grander than friendship, began to foster for those who had offered it to him.

As the day progressed, this feeling grew only stronger; for they were to him as clairvoyant servants, meeting every desire he'd ever known, satisfying every craving he'd concealed, and offering quelling to yearnings of which he had yet no knowledge.

Evening fell, and Lucius slapped Adam on the back, saying, "Son, I am overjoyed that you have come to stay with us! I do hope we have been able to make this first day of your stay comfortable."

"Most comfortable!" Adam declared. "I have never known such luxury! Why, the food, the music, the dancing, the recreation, the entertainment—for what more could a man ask?"

"Perhaps," Lucius replied, nodding as a smirk grew upon his face, "just one more thing."

"What's that?"

"You're a young man," he said, taking Adam under his arm and walking with him across the room. "Go," he whispered, tilting his head subtly toward the staircase. "She's waiting for you."

Lucius then gently grasped and lifted Adam's hand.

In it he placed a room key.

He then took his leave, saying not another word.

Adam watched him go; the feeling of having just walked into a door was rather potent.

Did he mean…?

Gazing up the towering set of stairs, a small tremor infected his muscles.

Did he *really* mean…?

Adam had always been the confident type, the kind who would never hesitate to dive headfirst into a new adventure. But this long-desired adventure had caught him completely by surprise; it really had hit him as a door set in his path—seemingly out of nowhere. Long had he danced about the fire, toying with the flames, reveling in the sparks and waves of radiant, rippling heat, even daring once in a while to let the rampage singe a hair or two—but no more than that. Now…he felt himself drenched in gasoline.

Is she…?

Dolores.

What woman could compare with her?

Was this really happening?

Wetting his lips with his dried tongue, Adam extended his quaking hand to the railing; it leapt up and down upon the wooden post as if on a trampoline, before his strength finally aided in clasping the support.

And, so, he climbed.

Every footfall fell weaker than the last; every step saw his legs rumble and wobble all the more; until at last he reached the top on all fours and crawled to the room on which was nailed a number to match the one attached to the key he'd been given: number four.

Pausing there on the floor to calm his breathing and bolster his resolve, Adam closed his eyes and grit his teeth; and into his head there flashed something he did not expect: Nothing.

Rising to his feet, Adam inserted his key and slowly turned the doorknob.

Stepping inside, he beheld, seated upon the end of the bed, the figure of Dolores. At first glance, she appeared exactly as she had earlier in the day; but as a shadow fell over her eyes, a smile was slowly painted across her face, and the gentle angel he had beheld was suddenly transformed into a titanic force, compelling and ponderous, beyond his willfully dwindling capacity to resist. Her willowy frame rose like a ribbon caught in a gentle, warm breeze, and her long, dark hair rippled like waves on a midnight ocean, tossed about in the swirling atmosphere of the spinning room, as she glided slowly toward him; every step, though as soft as a butterfly's, shook violently the very ground on which he stood, until Adam, hardly able to breathe, surrendered his control and fell hard to the floor at Dolores' feet.

Face to the ground, he gasped for air, then lifted his eyes to behold the beauty towering above him; but those eyes were stopped as they passed over her feet. Bare, he saw upon each of them a tattoo. Magnificent pieces of art, they were—crafted by expert hands, no doubt. And he lowered his face to them that he might perceive every detail with absolute clarity.

On the right foot had been drawn a bucking horse, standing proudly, as if readying to march forth at the head of a parade waiting close behind. Its shape was lined in black, though its body had not been painted; thus, it was made as pale as the porcelain skin on which it had been etched. Though he wondered if his eyes had invented it, he perceived the shape of a letter A in the steed's hind legs, formed as its swishing tail passed behind them, cutting across their centers; and in the horse's front legs, one of which fell straight, while the other bent beside it, he wondered if he was beholding a letter D.

Turning his attention to the left foot, he saw a very detailed jawless skull painted black, bearing an upper row of wild, jagged teeth. Upon these his eyes were called to gaze a second time; for what had at first met the eye as mere teeth were seen now as twisted letters of an archaic hand; and in this collection, arranged from the left to the right and bookended by a pair of 𝔐s, were the following: 𝔒, 𝔯, 𝔗, 𝔈.

Adam had not another breath.

Just then, a delicate hand reached down and cupped his chin, lifting his head and drawing his body upward. When at last he had found his feet, Dolores took him by the nape, pulled him nearer, and breathed inaudibly into his ear. And as she coiled her arms about him, Adam realized that he was no longer wearing his backpack.

***

Adam spent the night shivering in the rain, somewhere far beyond the hotel, at a distance determined only by what strength his running legs could muster before failing completely.

It had been a quick search for his backpack; someone seemed to have felt it would be best stored in a dumpster behind the hotel. While discovering it had indeed been a relief, Adam, who had also managed to avoid running into Lucius upon bolting down the stairs and out the door, wondered why, as he sat there in the rain, finding this darned backpack had been such a big deal to him at the time—a most urgent business it had been, locating this missing gift from Bear, even though he had not yet so much as touched the map sealed within. Even now his eyes had yet to behold its presence; yet, he somehow just knew the map was still zipped inside. And, so, acting upon this, he fumbled about in the dark for the zipper handle that he might at last take in hand Bear's answer to the questions of "Where?" and "How?"

Reaching inside the bag, Adam lifted, to his surprise, a thick book; he had expected something more akin to a scroll or a tri-fold. Through the dark and rain, Adam strained to see what directional etchings the map contained; but page after page, Adam gleaned naught but vexation. Indeed he saw words, but their order was strange, frustrating—nonsensical, even; foolishness, to be sure. Though dark, the bodies of each letter were clear as day, forming words in proper orders; they could be read from left to right in sentences, couplets, stanzas, and paragraphs. And each, individually and when combined, formed the lines of a map. Still, how could this be correct, thought he? For there are no such roads in this world, are there?

No—something must be wrong, here.

Perhaps, he considered, if he read it another way, the picture would make more sense.

He gave the book a quarter turn, then another.

Immediately, as if by Magic, his eyes beheld something a great deal more familiar.

These, he declared, were the roads he knew!

Onward he read, page after page, until he was so sure of his way that he contemplated tossing the map into the mud. In no short time, however, he thought better of this—perhaps he'd like to reference it once more, somewhere down the road. And, reasoning thusly, he gathered himself to his feet and proceeded on his way, all the while wondering, in the very same manner as he had when fleeing the hotel: What was this odd tugging presently urging him to retain the map, the exact same tugging that had yanked him from Dolores' bedroom?

***

"I said deal me in again, darn you!"

"And I said you ain't got no way to buy a new hand!"

"Same as always, Speck! I pay with my winnings!"

"Yeah, sure. I got IOUs falling out of my pockets—no deal, boy!"

Adam had lost all track of time, place, and purpose.

When it was could not be told.

Where it was could not be named.

And *why* it was had no meaning whatsoever.

"Speck, c'mon! I *need* to play another hand. I can't walk outta here with nothing again—no, no; not again; *no*, I can't!"

"Oh, *no*? Guess you should'a kept that in mind before you dropped your last coin onto the table and into my pocket. Get lost, *bum*!"

"Wait! No! Speck! Pl—"

No sooner had Adam leapt onto the table did a thoroughly annoyed Speck deliver the ratty, filthy drifter a smart blow to the cheek, sending him toppling onto the floor with a noisy crash that not only drew a cry from Adam's desperate lips, but also dislodged an ace of clubs from within his ragged sleeve.

"Well, well, boys," came a wicked and devilishly pleased chuckle from beneath Speck's wide and wild eyes; there was, in the sound slithering off his tongue, a sense of being quite beyond irritated with the situation, mixed with a sort of gleeful note or tone, born of the promise that a deep and festering itch had just been offered a finger by which to be scratched. "Seems our little *player* isn't yet through playing games."

Like a helpless, condemned peasant lying in the midst of a coliseum, surrounded by thousands upon thousands of wild spectators cheering for his demise, while a pack of ravenous lions closes in about him, Adam could smell the ghostly presence of Death nearing; so noisome was its stench, even his tongue could sense it. The air, sucked in massive gulps into his lungs, was like murky clouds of dust filled with fine needles that pricked and punctured his lungs from within. His head spun wildly, frantically, scanning every direction for an escape or helping hand, but neither could be found. The ground beneath him seemed to have crumbled into an abyss of nothingness; every sight and sound seared his heart with permanent brandings from the iron of Fear; his mind could hardly process the moments that flashed before him, as not one image his gaping eyes drank against their will dared linger long in his head.

Just then, a set of mighty fists, like two bolts of lightning, were hurled into his chest with bone-breaking force; and before he could catch his breath, he found his body ascending with great speed, until he was hovering over the giant man that was Speck, affixed to him by those same two fists.

"Take a good look, boys!" Speck laughed as he jostled about like a prized kill of wild game Adam's stunned and impotent body. "See here—he who'd had it all! The prodigal prince!"

A deafening roar of laughter filled the space, as to every mind came the image of the young man who had once, many years ago, waltzed through their doors, dripping with wealth and women, fame and fun, revelry and recklessness; the one who had indeed had it all, it seemed, and prodigally pillaged his own pockets for the flavors of Now and Much. How common was he, in point of fact, so like the many surrounding him: both celebrated and forgotten, known and unknown; but how pathetic he looked now: an exalted commoner, brought beneath the tier of low, with his fancy clothes replaced with tattered rags, and his well-groomed and perfumed exterior replaced with something like a barren, rotting tree, emitting a stench like the remnant of the slop that has long since passed through the bellies of pigs.

"Our nobody wants to be *distinguished* once more! Shall we oblige him?"

So much like a thorn had Adam been in the lives of those who had once adored him, so much like a blemish standing proudly upon the tip of the nose, that in this query was found for the crowding mass something akin to restitution and relief—they cheered; triumphantly they cheered, those he might have once called friends. Some cheered with glee, others with fury; they cheered their approval, their urgent approval.

Turning his fiery eyes to Adam's petrified face, Speck—holding still high in the air the quaking lad, only now by a single fist—dug a hand into his pocket and retrieved a switchblade. One terrifying *click* later, Adam's eyes were blinded by the glint bounding off of a long, silver razor dancing tauntingly before his face.

Still breathless from Speck's tremendous blow, Adam could not summon strength enough to wiggle even one of his limbs—regardless, his arms were presently trapped at his sides, held firmly by two men oozing wicked giggles through their teeth.

But as the blade began to slowly seep into and crawl through the flesh of his cheek, a spasm of desperation burst through him; and, directing it to one of his legs, Adam delivered a freeing kick to Speck's groin.

Upon impact with the floor, Adam pleaded with his rattled brain to stop tossing about the room that he might make for the door, while somewhere behind him in the spinning world there erupted a violent roar of rage and pain. Finding his feet, Adam made a blind dash through tables, chairs, and bodies, aiming for the blur of light just ahead. And he could just barely taste the cool, eventide air when something like a freight train slammed into his side.

"HOLD HIM!"

Though somewhere between the present and the void, Adam recognized the scream echoing in his ringing ears as belonging to a Speck radiating more ire than ever he had known the man to possess.

Again and again that voice hollered, rising from a great distance and racing nearer with every rabid syllable, until at last those words rained over him from directly above. So cacophonous did reality become that Adam could no longer distinguish words from sound. All that could be sensed was the wetness running over his face. When the first drop hit, it made a startling impact; it was cold, bubbly, stringy, and runny. Several more drops like this one followed. And then came a shattering pain; it exploded outward from the very center of his face, the epicenter, and seared every nerve as it rippled all the way to the back of his skull.

Not long thereafter, a new, terribly warm wetness began to stream over his face.

As the epicenter pulsed, exploding over and over again, more and more streams emerged to wet his cheeks, lips, and forehead; and from this branching river of warmth, which became frigid and dry the further it drifted, was produced even more rain, as great waves were from it formed by the repeated explosions: great crested waves throwing showers even over his eyes.

The taste of Death was so potent now, its poison so thick and filling his gaping mouth, clogging his throat, that Adam threw his eyes into the void above to find and offer himself freely unto oblivion. But then, ever so suddenly, he heard a great cry, one like the burst of sunlight through a heavy rain cloud, carried on a voice presently foreign, yet familiar in memory—it silenced the roar of the violent crowd and liberated Adam from the chains holding him to the floor.

Overriding his forfeit, Adam's body snatched the reins and set his limbs into a gallop. On all fours he sped into the fading light of sunset, over grass, rocks, and dirt, until he collapsed in a patch of mud and water so far from the footprint of man that naught but the restless rummaging of insects could be heard.

He could breathe only through his mouth, and there was not one spot on his face that did not scream in agony. What burned all the more, however, was the indignity of it all—the injustice, even! That he had been thoroughly pummeled was one thing— and no small thing, whatsoever; but the chief item on his grow-ing-by-the-second list of gratuitous sufferings and severe griev-ances was the fact that his last possession, save for the clothes on his back (which not even he could covet), had been stolen in a hand of cards.

While Adam had come to care very little for his backpack (and even less for the map therein), the thought of it being in Speck's hands infuriated him. Adam would have sold the backpack and its contents for a song—less, even, than that; a whistle, perhaps, or a hum! But he would have died before losing to the very image of abhorrence that which he despised in neglect—surely, he could think of no token so grand or scrap of refuse so repugnant that he would not be loath to lose to such a creature as Speck.

And, so, still clinging to life, Adam, peering through the one eye that was yet of normal size and not hidden beneath a bubble of puffy skin, climbed from the mud by cover of midnight and began a slow crawl to the roadhouse whence he'd fled.

Now, if you will pardon me, dear reader (and I hope I judge rightly at present in concluding that you will), I shall skip briskly over Adam's painfully slow journey to the aforementioned roadhouse; for it is indeed a story filled only with pain and slowness. He crawled and groaned and groaned and crawled—this, I sincerely hope, will suffice to carry you on to the next step in Adam's journey. If not, might I suggest you pause and repeat for the next hour or so the pre-colon part of the latter sentence, that you might truly experience, and maybe even share in, the toil and suffering of that over which (and with all sanity intact) I and the not-a-masochist-reader shall presently bound.

A lonely streetlamp burned, illuminating the door of the roadhouse. Nothing stirred in any direction. Darkness cloaked the surrounding nothing along the single road leading only here; it was as lonely a dirt road as the one on which he and the inhabitants of the roadhouse before him did tread. And, crossing this dead-end way, Adam slipped into the shadows in which it slumbered, and there scoured for a means of entry.

Being that it was the height of summer, Adam looked not long for an open window; and, being also that he yet carried just enough weight to be identified by a bathroom scale as a sickly feather, he found the surge of adrenaline—mixed with rage, indignation, and a determination to attain justice—to be more than sufficient to lift his body up a drainpipe and to a dark opening on the second floor. A pre-summer Adam, thought he as he climbed through the window, might have been left at the bottom, flat on his backside, with all the determination in the world burning in his heart and a rusty drainpipe in his hands—a blessing, perhaps, was this present constitution, wrought by this suffering.

Now inside, Adam widened his good eye in an effort to make known the secrets of the dark. After some time spent adjusting, he found that he was indeed in one of the bunkrooms, just not Speck's. Feeling about, so as to not crash into an obstruction and identify his presence to the nearby sleeper, Adam made his way for the door. But as he did so, his carefully feeling hands touched down on something like a soft blanket; and when he paused to better examine the object, he found the disrobed robes of the man snoring just above him. Adam's mission had been to recover his backpack; but here, in his hands, lay something surely more valuable.

In a flash, he'd made up his mind; and, a few flashes later, he was at the door to the hallway, his filthy, ratty robes heaped in his wake in the exact spot he'd discovered his new outfit.

Turning carefully the doorknob, he made for the hall.

Still crawling, Adam searched every room for Speck and the stolen backpack; but both were nowhere to be found. What had been found in the exploration of each room, however, were many sets of trousers belonging to those who had stolen his money and bruised his body. He could not without making known his presence take any vengeance for his flesh; so, he settled for making amends for the negative balance in his bank account via the money stuffed in their pockets.

Carrying now a great deal more weight in paper and coin, Adam, still hungry to find Speck, crawled to the stairs; and, having made his descent, he came upon the main room, wherein he found a black stain near the door, like a splat of spilt paint, and the sound of heavy breathing coming from within the distant darkness.

There…

If that heavy breathing belonged to Speck, as he so hoped it did, venturing into the darkest corner he'd yet explored—over wood floors perhaps more restless and whiny than those above ("Due to greater use, maybe?" said he, pausing for a moment of internal supposition)—would surely make the recovery of his backpack a more appreciated effort, and whatever additional money collected all the more earned.

Adam began his crawl.

He was now so conscious of his sound production that he wondered if it were possible to prop himself up on ten fingers and ten toes, and scuttle as if on crab's legs across the treacherous terrain. No sooner did that thought cross his mind did a most ornery splinter of wood leap from a floorboard and dig its fang (which, I suppose, would also be its face—or, to be fair, the splinter could have been resting face down, feet high, making the piercing end its feet; unless, of course, the nature of the splinter species is such that all elements that make up the body are one and undistinguished, in which case it would be foolish to suggest a fragmented piece of treated tree hide would even have a face or feet. And now I must also wonder, are floorboards actually tree *hide*? Or, would it be tree flesh, or tree body? Where were we?).

Right.

The splinter.

So, dear reader, the time I spent lost on a tangent equals in approximate measuring the amount of time Adam had been deprived of breath following his encounter with the splinter. Every muscle contracted as the always-surprising agony brought about by surface-level nerve slicings raced through his body like an out-of-control freight train. Though he made no noise—a feat accomplished with not a little effort—his contorting face mimed every sound and articulated every vile word he so desperately wanted audibly to produce.

When at last the hysteria had subsided, Adam rolled over onto his back and carefully began to dislodge the nasty shard. As he did so, his mind began to wonder if Speck was even still in the house—it was, he thought, just as likely that Speck had departed as it was that he was sleeping in the very corner of the room where their earlier brawl had begun.

The splinter now removed, Adam contemplated abandoning his mission. But, he quickly reasoned, he had already crossed half of the floor to the heavy breather in the dark. If indeed it were Speck, Adam would not let the blackguard meet the morning with *his* backpack in hand. And that's exactly where he found the backpack: in Speck's hand.

As it turns out, the heavy breather in the dark had been correctly identified—what was more, he had a wad of cash stuffed carelessly and loosely in his top pocket. Making quick work of Speck's money, Adam moved to relieve him of the backpack, the strap of which was coiled about his fingers and locked in a fist.

It was so dark that Adam's one good eye, though well adjusted by now, could draw little from the pitch before it, other than, basically, an outline. He spent some time examining Speck's hand from every angle, until at last he determined it was either give up or get started, and hope Speck is as heavy a sleeper as he is a breather.

He began.

The first finger (the littlest piggy) peeled away nicely.

No resistance.

No stirring.

So far, so good.

Adam advanced upon the next three (the swine known respectively for staying home, having roast beef, and being denied a portion of that roast beef), taking each at once, as the backpack's strap was looped over the ring and index fingers, and pressed tightly beneath the middle.

Though he had never done so, Adam felt as though he were in the midst of diffusing a bomb.

Scooting closer to Speck, Adam carefully lifted the backpack and set it in his lap; then, as gently as his trembling fingers could muster, he slowly began to slip it free, pausing only when Speck's heavy breathing was interrupted by a belch or a tick, or when any of his fingers would twitch.

At long last, Adam had liberated his backpack—as it turned

out, the thumb had not been involved, possibly due to its having been engaged elsewhere as a hog gone to market.

And now the time had come to go.

Adam, rising to his feet, backpack in hand and money in pockets, he loomed over the shadow-saturated face of Speck, while a violent brew boiled within. He so wished the present circumstance were different—something along the lines of Adam having in his possession a giant club or maybe even a knife (he'd looked for Speck's switchblade, but couldn't find it in any of his pockets). And, so, with a tremendous gamble on the deepness of Speck's slumber, Adam drew himself up and hurled a gob of spit into what he hoped was Speck's eye.

Turning his good eye to the door, Adam crossed the creaking boards without a care; he didn't even shut the door upon exiting. How could he have done, when the knob was ten feet down?

***

Just about the time the wolves had ceased their howling at the moon, Adam let out his first of many howls at the rising sun.

Lying in the muddy earth, Adam wailed and cried with sounds that squeezed his tired lungs and shred his throat, as he gazed in disbelief and horror at a red-speckled shard of white breaking through his skin and pant leg, just above the knee. Everything below that knee was upside down—as was his back, his shin and toes were imbedded into the mud, while his calf faced the sky. The suddenness of the fall, and the agony in which his rapid descent had resulted, had left him rather unaware as to how exactly he'd ended up this way—the tremendous pain also offered no help to his functions of reason and recollection. However, given that I am a practicing Omniscient, I, dear reader, can relate to you precisely how our leading man had come to be in such an unfortunate state.

The woods have soft tongues, but we omniscient narrators have large ears.

Shuffling about through the dark, his backpack recovered and spoils jingling merrily in his pockets, Adam's feet began quickly and more confidently (an adjective better translated by the levelheaded as "carelessly") to *pitter-patter* through an ocean of black. It had been an exhilarating night (or, early morning), and with all his heart he wanted to dash through the woods like a gazelle, to feel the rush of the moment amplified in even wilder beatings of his heart; to make real, if only for a moment, the sensation of flight with every leap and bound. But the woods are treacherous, given its many inhabitants and its most dominant and name-inspiring group's proclivity for stretching their branches however they darn well please. So, with arms fully extended, he kept to a brisk trot with perhaps a bit too much faith in what he was increasingly believing was a newfound and potent ability to sense without the employment of the eyes obstructive and potentially disagreeable objects lurking in the dark.

His focus remained fixed upon what this supposed Magical sense and hyperextended appendages could tell; until the jingling noise rising from his pockets suddenly diverted his attention.

Though he did not stop, he wondered if it would be wiser to utilize the backpack to store his midnight earnings, that he might centralize the weight and enclose the numerous pieces, thus avoiding the lamentable loss of even one coin to the earthly abyss. But before he could unzip the bag to make the transfer, his lack of focus on his feet finally collided with consequence: somewhere within the pool of black through which he ran, the earth had disappeared completely; and, helplessly throwing his weight into this pit of nothing, Adam fell like a feather tied to an anvil through pure, untouched night, until a collection of tree roots snatched his ankle out of mid air, leaving the rest of his body to continue its fall without his cemented leg.

Nearly the same moment the woods became filled with a gunshot-like *CRACK*, Adam's spinning body landed with about as hard and breathtaking a *WUMP* as Gravity will perform on a poor soul it has decided at the last second to preserve amongst the living.

It would take until the sun began to rise for Adam to recover enough breath to scream; in the meantime, he could but writhe and gasp and weep and vomit, his mind lost in a whirlwind of agony and madness. But, when at last he did regain an adequate lung capacity for the task, he wailed with such violence that the ground quaked, the trees splintered, and his enemies were swiftly beckoned.

"This boy sure is one persistent mess, ain't he?"

Thrice the earth rumbled.

"And what's this?"

TINK

"You know, I was *wondering* where all my cash had gone!"

"There's more in his pockets!"

"Those ain't *his* pockets, are they?"

"HEY! He's wearing my clothes!"

"Glad to see you're finally joining the party—of course they're your clothes! I *told* you it had to have been him! I told you he was the one who'd taken everything! Idiot left his own rags lying about like a calling card!"

"What's wrong with his eyes?"

"I'll bet I can fix 'em—hang on a second."

A pain like boiling acid enveloping the body, like rusted razors being scraped along his nerves; a pain that made the cup of Death appear as a bubbling fountain of wine roared like white flame through Adam's entire body; and instantly his eyes dropped out of his head and fixed their gaze upon a snarling, wild-faced Speck, standing at his side with a hand clamped about and twisting the bone sticking through Adam's pants.

"See? Fixed 'em! Good morning, Adam!"

The sound falling at a snail's sprint over Speck's lips was nearly as searing as the pain still screeching through his body.

"Think you got something that belongs to us," chuckled Speck, finally releasing the bone and walking slowly toward Adam's head. Kneeling, he placed his lips firmly against Adam's ear, and whispered, "A *few* things, actually."

With the speed of a bullet, Speck's bloodstained hand snatched a hold of Adam's jaw, while the two burly men that had accompanied him began stripping Adam of their stolen money and clothes.

"It's a dark, dark world, Adam," whispered Speck as the morning chill began biting Adam's exposed skin. "And we are all but blind rats, clawing about in our own filth, desperate to claw another day. We eat the filth to buy the dawn. Fools, all of us."

His body now completely stripped, the two men began mercilessly beating and kicking him; all the while Speck held fast to Adam's jaw with pulverizing strength.

"I couldn't care less whether you live or die," Speck continued, speaking now with an eerie calm. "But I will not hesitate to rip the fangs from any foolish rat that nibbles on *my* pile of filth. ENOUGH!"

Having lifted his head, Speck shouted thusly and the beating ceased.

Turning his eyes once more to his thoroughly broken and terrified victim, Speck scooped a handful of mud and brutishly stuffed it into Adam's mouth, breaking some of Adam's teeth and cutting his own hand against a few others.

"FEED, RAT!" he screamed, looming over Adam with a maniacal mien pouring forth a dark and throaty laughter, brewed in the depths beyond the physical realm and consuming all it touched in the terror of its essence, while his mighty hands, like bear traps, clamped shut Adam's mouth, and his eyes, like the mouths of sister peaks erupting in unison, bleeding over his blue-faced prey the full measure of his wicked delight.

After a great deal of choking and expelling mud through is nostrils, Adam's mouth was released with a vicious shove.

Speck rose to his feet and watched Adam vomit the mud back into the earth.

"What's this?"

In turning to leave, Speck was handed what one of the others had found nearby: a backpack.

"Ah, yes," he chuckled with a derisive snort. "A poor winning for such a good hand." Holding it aloft for a moment, Speck gave the backpack a quick shake; and, deciding its nearly weightless weight meant it was empty, he threw it to the ground beside Adam's head, saying, "What a waste of a full house."

With one final look of revulsion at the pathetic boy, lying naked and crying in the mud, Speck spat in his face and disappeared.

***

He had never known the summer sun to be so cruel, or the days of sunshine to be so dark.

On his belly he crawled, as he had the day before, and the day before that, and every night in between; through each and every day—a countless parade of them, it seemed—he crawled like a beast, crying and moaning, feeding only upon that which his weak hands could reach: worms, grubs, spiders, and ants; grass, leaves, and dirt. Dragging his dead and mangled leg behind him—the bone now as black as the mud, and his wound painted grisly colors most eyes, if they could stand to behold it, would call unnatural—he sought roads upon which many feet did tread. And from their shoulders he would call to passersby, pleading, begging for salvation; but no one gave him anything: not a hand, not a glance; he was no more human in their story than the dirt beneath their feet.

Every time, he watched them go—he'd watch each one until the distance consumed them. What little hope he had was stretched thin by desperation; but with every new face that came his way, he saw naught but a single, familiar design: a face he'd known well, so very long ago, one he had adored more than anything in the world; a face that defined the only thing that mattered: a face that was his own. Seeing his face painted on every person passing above him was a dagger in the heart of Hope.

And, so, he wandered, blistering beneath the merciless sun, with no real direction, point, or purpose.

There seemed no way and nowhere to go.

Nowhere.

Except…

Here, in his hour of desperation, of ultimate hopelessness and humility like a mountain crushing him underfoot, Adam could think of but one word: Home.

That word had been a twisting in his stomach, a revolting thought, a nauseating institution, and an unthinkable destination; once departing, he had vowed never to return to the house of his father, so long as he had breath in his lungs. Indeed, these had been his exact words; together, they had been a promise made inwardly and with iron fervency.

But now, with very little breath left to spare, his iron will melted, and his pride mortally wounded, Adam could think of nothing more comforting, nothing safer, and nothing so sure to again make the world right than the arms of his father.

It had been a long and terribly painful journey, during which his pride became ever more like the dust on which he fed. But every speck of residue from the many sufferings had along the way was dispelled the moment he saw the house of his youth on the dawning horizon.

Though he could still but crawl, Adam's body felt as though it had taken flight, and what would be hours passed in mere minutes.

Just before the sun had reached the apex of its climb, Adam's hand fell upon the stones on which he'd once ridden his first bicycle; and as the sun filled his eyes, his fingers caressed the grass in which his father had taught him how to catch and throw, where they'd wrestled until their clothes were stained green, where they had lain beneath the stars and marveled at the designs painted in the heavens. His father's land was yet rich, both in wealth and memory.

At last, he was home.

Adam resumed his crawling, making for the door. As he did so, a single, lonely cloud, the only one in the heavens that day, passed over the sun; and as it did, the light that had filled Adam's eyes was banished, and he looked in horror at what was so much more than the work of the hands of Time.

What stones he had felt beneath his palms had been pulverized to dust; grass that had danced between his fingers had been taken by the weeds, the rich soil made like the face of a desert. The grand house he had seen on the horizon was but a doorframe, its door opened to a pile of rubble and debris that had once been comfort, security, and home.

The air around him pressed against his body like the arms of a vice; he could draw not breath enough to cry, nor could his body find the strength to drag himself to the front door to see the terrible price that had been paid. And, so, sealing his eyes and closing his heart, that what elements of destruction might be ignored and forgotten, Adam turned and made a blind path to somewhere, anywhere—it didn't matter where; anywhere but here. But he would crawl only a short distance before his head collided with a rather stubborn obstruction that toppled his tired body and forced his eyes to open.

HERE LIES...

He could read but one line more—a name of old, bound to his very being—before his eyes sealed once again, while his grief, proving far more mighty than the vice still clutching him, burst forth with wails and sobs, crippling him all the more; and, falling upon his father's grave, he watered the dry and fractured ground that had known not the kiss of rain since the day the earth had reclaimed the man buried beneath.

Adam was broken.

At long last, he had reached the end.

The dusty path forged by his hands had borne no fruit; only Death could here be found.

He was sorry for his existence, for what he had done with it, how he had used it; he was sorry not as one who is caught in the midst of his transgression, nor as one without an alternate feeling remaining, having spent the rest in exasperation; rather, he was actively sorry: he wept remorse, on bitter guilt he fed and was rendered empty; contrition as never he'd known it was made clear and right in his mind—how deeply he understood the cost of his life's work. More than anything else, however, Adam was sorry for those upon whose paths he had tread; that there had been even *one* person whose life had, without just cause, been irreparably polluted by the toxicity that was his existence—*this* was a guilt and grief beneath which he was sure he would be justly crushed. And with only the feeble quaking in his hands to mobilize them for action, he tore at the earth, seeking there to imbed his hands, reclaim the dead, and in his stead assume his own rightful place.

Before the sun could dry the river of tears that cut across the fractured ground before the weathered headstone, Adam had turned toward the road, resolved to spare his father any further contamination by his own presence, and be thereafter (and in some distant and forgotten place) swallowed whole by the earth. Thus, he went to seek the robe of Death, somewhere along the dusty road. But as his fingers touched down upon the path, his face fell onto a set of dusty boots.

"My, my—look who it is!"

Adam knew that voice.

Had it crashed against him several hours prior, his wish for relief from the sun's merciless heat might have been granted in the turning of his blood to ice; but Adam was now well beyond any regard for feeling.

"What in the world happened to *you*? The *world*, perhaps?"

As a taunting chuckle filled the air, a set of very soft hands descended and turned Adam onto his back.

Blinded by the unobstructed sun, Adam could not see the face of him who stood above; though, he could perceive it in vivid detail.

"You owe me something, lad," whispered the voice.

Adam could hear the voice's origin kneeling beside him. And then, a giant head floated slowly over his, eclipsing the sun; and as glowing rays of gold wrapped the head in a halo, the face of Lucius came into view.

"Look at you," he sneered with a disgusted shake of the head. "Nose broken, face scarred, naked and feeble, feted and filthy, broken and twisted—I'd offered you *much* more than this." The baritone choir that was Lucius' voice suddenly became like a rumbling storm cloud. "And you repay me by slipping away into the night without paying—even slighting my daughter, whom I'd offered to you as a comfort! You threw away my kindness— the opulence and repose I alone offer the undeserving; you threw it all away for a world of suffering! How like a fool! But I will see your debt paid," he growled; the storm was becoming restless, ready to explode at any moment. "I *WILL* see you reap your wages forever in *MY* house!"

With that, Lucius lifted from his boot a dagger; and, raising it high, he threw it with crushing force toward Adam's chest.

At last, the time had come to die, thought Adam; and with a sigh of regretful thanks, and with full acceptance of the justice sailing swiftly against his existence, he sealed his eyes.

Lying there, now at the threshold of oblivion, so soon after dawning from it, Adam saw clearly his every step, from the first to the last; and know them he did as never he'd known anything. He saw their origins and consequences, and everything that lay in between, all in an instant; intimately he knew and understood them, and not one did he see worth saving, nor could one be found strong enough to save him. What he had seen at his father's grave had been the broad stroke of the brush; seeing now the marks of every single bristle made him all the more grateful he would soon poison no longer even so much as the least of the grains of dust on which he lay. And when at last the whole parade of his existence had shown its ultimate end, Adam, hopeless and alone, cried out for a mercy he could not name, but hoped so desperately might hear him, might know him, and be willing to rescue him from the blow to come, and from the clutches of Death he had so ignorantly desired and now feared with all his being.

It was then that Adam realized that his accuser's knife was taking quite a while to fall; and, moments later, his eyes were awakened to the sight of Lucius wailing wildly in agony as he was crushed between a set of powerful arms, his dagger casting forth the face of its handle toward the heavens, its blade buried within a mighty chest, cutting deeply through Bear's tender heart.

***

Adam could hear not his own scream, though every fiber in his body did tremble at the sound.

Lucius had been made like the dust of the road, and there in its midst, at the convergence of two opposite paths, lay Bear, his blood painting the way.

Crawling to his side and climbing up his massive chest, as if it were a mountain, Adam fell upon this foe of old, sobbing well beyond his control, with great heaves and countless tears, more numerous than the gentle raindrops that began to fall amid the sunshine. And though it was he who lay dying, 'twas Bear did rise to hold and uphold Adam's weak and broken body.

"Eyes ahead, son," whispered Bear, his voice strong, but fading. And, taking from the dirt road the backpack he'd given Adam in a time that seemed so distant as to have been several lifetimes past, he unzipped the bag, and gently took Adam's tired and tattered hands and placed them inside.

His fingers coiled about the map therein, and, with Bear's strength to carry his arms, it was lifted into the light. Regarding the map as last he had in the dark, Adam beheld now as upside down and backward words that had once seemed easier to comprehend and simpler to follow. And as his mind struggled to grasp the reason why that which had governed and compelled his walking through the world appeared now as so confused an orientation and erratic a route, Bear's mighty hand grasped the map and gently gave it a quarter turn, and then another. By the light of day, by all that had transpired, by all with which he had been blessed, the words and their order suddenly began to make sense, so much so that he felt as if he were looking through a brand new set of eyes. As clear as the dawn reflected in a crystal pool, and even more so, he read from left to right in sentences, couplets, stanzas, and paragraphs; and each, individually and when combined, formed the lines of a map that was most alive—vibrant, active; it cut through his flesh, bone, and sinews to his very being and made known the way in which he should go.

Adam looked up into Bear's giant face. How his heart did break when first he saw a grisly scar cutting across Bear's cheek, just below the eye, reminding Adam of what he had done, how he had once hoped with all his strength to be as the knife stealing now the life of his deliverer. But before his gaze could part and fall to the earth in shame and despair, that which sat above the scar snatched it back and pulled it upward, where he beheld a set of enormous eyes, brighter than the sun shining amid the rain. As if in them was no memory of wrongs past, these eyes beamed back at him, *swalla*-ing him whole, and then beckoned Adam's gaze to follow his outstretched arm to a single point beyond an extended sausage finger.

Looking forth, Adam perceived a long and narrow road of rich soil, cutting through and shattering the wide and dusty road on which he'd crawled; 'twas the road on which Bear had set him long (yet, not so long) ago. And as the rain washed over him, cleansing his skin and soothing its suffering, Adam felt Bear's mighty arms close about him; and there in that embrace, he rested.

***

The rain did fall, still through the open sunshine; there was not a cloud in the sky.

In the rich soil where he lay, at the crossroads, Adam buried the man he now called a friend: once the most hated image, thought, sound, and idea in his mind, Bear had become the greatest of what Adam had never truly known. And though he wept as he dug, his hands the only tools with which to claw at the earth, his sorrows were soon banished by a joy he could not understand, as well as a burning, iron will to forge ahead.

With a kiss to the earth, Adam turned to face the road. Though the horizon appeared hazy from where he stood, the path was clear. Nothing between his ears, nor any sensation tossing about in his chest, could tell where the path would lead. Perhaps, thought he, a road such as this could be navigated with a map.

Taking up the gift his friend had both bestowed and taught him how to read, Adam submitted himself to the gleaning, studying, and storing in heart and mind the direction found therein, the very path down which it called him to tread. And, in that way, he made his first step off the dusty path.

***

"Well, I'll tell you, son, you were in a right state—a mighty right state, indeed—last time I saw you! Glad to see you're perking up a bit!"

"Excuse me, sir…well, I—I don't mean to be rude, or anything, but…who are you?"

A great roar of jolly laughter filled the small room.

"Not surprised you don't remember! Why, you were sure in a daze, you were! The name's Liam, and *this*," he said, extending his arms proudly to the room, "along with *that*," he added, throwing a thumb through the open window, which looked out onto well-used grounds lined with barns and alive with all sorts of sounds, all bordering a field of golden wheat; "*this*," he said again, "is my farm."

The activity and sheer beauty of what lay just beyond the window called to Adam in such a way that he didn't realize he had started toward it.

"Whoa, now!" cried Liam, rushing to his side. "If you're gonna be getting up, you'll need my help—ain't got much life in that leg."

Adam at last took a moment to regard himself and his surroundings. He was lying in a large bed wrapped in snow-white sheets; his body was clean, his skin soft, and over it lay a nightgown like a feather cloud wrapped in a sweet, summer warmth, perfectly complementing the warm breeze blowing through the open window.

The room was small, but of an expert hand was its design; what craftsmanship had carved exposed joists, as well as all the furniture and even the trim about the window and lining the walls! Everything seemed to have been cut, carved, and placed by the bounty of a single, gigantic tree—indeed, it would not have surprised Adam to know that this dwelling lay in the bosom of the grandest, most glorious tree a man could behold.

"Let me help you, son," said Liam, cutting through Adam's tranced gazing.

Looking forth, Adam perceived Liam bowing with an outstretched hand, while the other held a set of wooden crutches. Taking the hand, Adam turned his eyes down to see his wounded leg wrapped tightly in bandages.

"Really something special, she is—probably saved that leg. C'mon, now; let's get that blood a-flowin'."

Adam's joints and muscles wailed in agony as he rose, but

he made no sound; there could be naught but joy to stand once again, much more even to be alive!

With Liam holding him firmly by the arm, Adam wobbled his way to the window, where, on a table just beside it, sat his backpack.

"There we go!" cheered Liam with a grunt and a beaming smile. "Beautiful day, isn't it?"

But Adam's eyes had fallen elsewhere.

"So!" Liam boomed as he gently draped an arm across Adam's shoulders. "What was it brought you out all this way?"

Adam stood silently for a moment, clutching what he had just a moment prior taken from the backpack. And then, turning his eyes to Liam, who had taken a curious note of the object in his hands, he tapped it thrice and said in a soft, hoarse voice as tears welled behind his eyes, "A gift from a friend."

Liam had not regarded the map for a full second before his face lightened, his grand smile becoming softer; and as a look of familiarity washed over him, Liam's eyes fell directly into Adam's.

"A gift unto us all," he said.

And with that, and one final pat on Adam's back, Liam took his leave.

***

Adam had not seen a mirror since the morning his summer journey had begun; and when into this mirror he did gaze, what gazed back at him was something he'd never seen in all his life.

Something like a beast, a bastardized recreation, a most violent rearranging of the familiar visage bore through him from the glass. Where once had been a bed of soft and smooth skin sat a fractured desert, littered with a chaotic mess of hideous lacerations, all forging confused paths, donning grotesque colors, and destined to be remembered long after their scabs had fallen. Where once had been chiseled features that had stolen glances and set many a young woman into a swoon sat now a rocky terrain, broken and misshapen, irreparably so. Where once had been something upon which he'd desired more than anything in the world to forever fix his eyes—a portrait in which to become blissfully lost, hanging neatly over a hollow vessel—sat now something he wished ne'er to see again, so long as he should live; something of which he hoped no one in the world would ever have to bear the misfortune of seeing.

But then, just as his fist rose to strike the beast staring back at him, he realized that a soul outside his own flesh had already beheld his hideous features without fear or disgust—more so, that soul had gazed with warming welcome and embracing excitement, as one greeting a most beloved friend.

Though Adam was not even remotely cured by this thought, another offered him peace for the time being: that perhaps now the portrait matched the vessel on which it hung: a hollow, fractured shell filled with refuse.

It was a just reality, thought he.

And how like his former self he would once again be: that he would bear a portrait in contrast to the vessel beneath; only now, that which was ugly would be that which is doomed anyway to perish, and that which endures could bear the marks and resemblance of a face and person not himself and wholly worthy of eternal, passionate captivation.

Adam spent several hours tottering to and fro about the room, getting used to his crutches, before dressing in the clothes lain neatly beside his bed. After some gleeful toil and happy suffering in stuffing his weak and pained body into fresh and benevolently provided attire (which also smelled the way spring feels), he made for the hall.

Every room was empty; it was just before sundown. But through the opened door were glorious sounds of jubilant commotion and blissful songs of celebration. And as he approached them, as the wind caught and lifted his limbs to know the life by which it whirled, he beheld a scene that to ancient eyes had been ordinary and lowly, erupting now in newness and beauty—*this*, thought he, is a place filled with true life.

All the chatterings of animals dancing and playing freely in the crisp, evening air were a heavenly chorus; every color boasted a vibrancy tenfold grander than that which its name could relate; even the air rushing about him caressed his skin with a richness like the taste of honey: it was full and smooth, and its whispers of a new land, free of the darkness of that which was no more, were like triumphant shouts of immeasurable joy.

Amid his relishing, he heard the voice of Liam calling to him.

"Out and about, I see! Wonderful!"

"Liam," said Adam on the wings of a breathless whisper, "you do indeed have a most beautiful place."

"These hands tend what they did not create, and I am a steward of what I do not own." Chuckling, he added, "I suppose I should stop referring to it as *my* farm, eh?"

"How does a man come to deserve something so wonderful as all this?"

"He doesn't, son; he can't."

"Surely," said Adam, looking Liam dead in the face, "you must have—"

"And I can tell you I haven't," Liam interrupted, casting an earnest gaze into Adam's eyes. "I learned long ago that these hands can't produce anything even remotely grander than the stuff I shovel out of the cattle stalls, day in and day out. What, then, can I say of all of this? To what must I bestow the credit? *Magic?*" Liam huffed with such force that Adam was surprised to not see the man's tonsils hurled forth to the ground. "No, son—it's what's in here," he said, tapping upon the map stuffed in Adam's hip pocket.

With a knowing, peaceful sigh, Adam surveyed the farm as it drifted softly to sleep beneath a blazing sunset.

"It sure is lovely, Liam," he breathed contentedly. "I'll never forget it."

Placing a hand on Adam's shoulder, Liam said, "Come; work the land with me. Let us share in this bounty—far too grand for the likes of me, it is. Work the land, and know its grand design and the voice alive within it; come, and know what even I yet discover—know it by every fiber that falls between your fingers and fills your senses to the brim with exactly that of which you and I can only hope to be made worthy."

Adam didn't need to think about it.

His hand fell almost instantly into Liam's.

"Good!" cheered Liam. "And tonight we celebrate!"

With that, Liam led Adam to his table; and when he began to set out three places, a word his host had spoken earlier leapt into his mind.

"Liam? Who is *she?* The she you'd mentioned earlier."

"*She*," Liam beamed—such a glow came about him as he spoke; one so grand that Adam could not help but marvel at the foreign reality that there could be such a radiance of abundant happiness as to render inadequate the very word used to describe it. "*She*," he said, "is the one whose healing touch, and years of experience fixing up the clumsiest of the livestock, probably helped to save that leg of yours—*AND*," he added, as the door slowly opened, "*she* is the one with the most incredible and incredibly impeccable timing! Adam, my boy," Liam proudly declared, sweeping forth a presentational hand, "this is my daughter, Aretina."

***

"It's like the 'e' in café."

"*Are-eh-tee-nah.*"

"You got it!"

"I'm glad you finally said something—a few more weeks pronouncing it your father's way and I might have been incapable of breaking the habit. I'll be sure to practice every night before bed—recite 'til I get it right."

"Do so, and you might get to know dad's shotgun a bit more intimately."

"But why does he say it that way?" Adam asked after recovering from a laugh. "I mean, wasn't it he who'd named you? Could it be that he's had it right all this time? *Air-ē-tee-nah?*"

"I think it's cute how he pronounces it; so, I don't bother to correct him."

Leaning forward, Aretina clutched her knees and gazed over the wheat field, wherein Liam was binding up his equipment for the night.

"It comes from my mother's name, actually," she said. "He called her Arie—so I've read, at least; that's what he's written on the back of her photographs. Her name was Ariel." Aretina's toes danced about lazily in the lush grass on which they sat; and as a soft and sad smile was painted across her face, she sighed, "I've often wondered if *that's* the reason he pronounces my name the way he does."

"He's never spoken of her," said Adam, watching closely the woman beside him, as she watched lovingly the man in the field nearby. "Not a word in all this time."

"He's said little more to me," she replied, turning her eyes into his. "I don't know if he's capable of *really* talking about her; though, I am sure she is ever with him, in heart and mind. No," she sighed, gazing back at her father, "he has said not one word in all my years to add to the picture of her I keep in my mind."

"How, then, did you come to learn anything at all about her?"

"When I was a girl, my father gifted me all she'd left behind: clothes, perfumes, brushes, keepsakes, trinkets; he also gave me every photograph he had of her, save for one; but of this treasure trove there was a single gift in particular that has been more of a mother to me than ever I've known: her diary."

Plucking a blade of grass, Aretina turned it about in her hand, musing, as if a beloved page of that diary had been etched upon it.

Adam dared not say a word.

"It's because of that diary I have come to wonder about my name," she continued. "One of her last entries talks about how she hopes the child within her will be a girl, whom she would name Christina, and call Tina for short. My father surely knew this wish; yet, I think he saw in me both a new gift and a reminder of a gift now gone; thus, he joined my given name with his bride's—and, here I am."

Adam, lying with his enchanted head propped up by and resting on his hand, fed upon her every word as if they were hearty servings of tender meat, while as wine he drank in the vision before him, set aglow by the ruby-golden sunset: long, umber waves, rippling like a playfully restless stream, framing heart-stopping eyes of the same variety; a vision like those artists of old had tried to capture in their masterpieces, yet had not the skill to weave nor the representative to model such angelic grace and beauty; a vision like the sound of the gentle wind, gliding sleepily o'er the fields of gold, or like the song of a mighty forest of everlasting green, dancing in the stillness of a soft and tranquil, midnight snowfall; a vision dressed in silks finer and more lovely than the wind-tossed meadows, the ones bellowing in brilliant colors buoyant bursts of ebullient laughter, yet, before her radiant hue, fell swiftly into reverent silence. A vision: near, yet too far away for hands such as his—imbued by the mire of the earth—to reach forth and touch. A vision: known by name, yet guarded in heart. A vision: the likes of which the world is unworthy even to bear the tread of her foot; yet, here she was, gazing willingly into his eyes. A vision, indeed, was she, and a gift; though, not for him.

"C'mon now, youngsters!" called Liam from the field. "High time we're getting indoors! Adam! Aretina! Let's get a-movin', now!"

"Well," said Adam, rising with no little difficulty to one knee. "I'll have to do some serious thinking about the pronunciation. *Air-ē-tee-nah* says he; *Are-eh-tee-nah* says you. However," he grunted, readying his wounded leg for the journey toward standing upright, "I might have to side with your father on this one, given that the name Ariel doesn't have the café 'e' sound."

Looking up at Adam with a soft, half-smile that was nothing more than a mask for the brighter smile within, Aretina spoke softly but resolvedly, "He may pronounce the name, but it is I who define it."

"That's good enough for me," Adam replied, his face unable to conceal a bright smile.

Aretina then lifted her arm, offering him her hand to be helped off the ground.

"Oh…um, well…I," Adam stammered, the smile in his cheeks replaced with a beet-like blushing; his eyes danced about his trembling, dirty hands, which extended and retreated before finally falling limp and defeated at his sides. Through a dejected sigh, he said at length, "I'm sorry, but I'm afraid my hands are just too dirty from working in the fields."

Aretina set free her bright smile, took firmly Adam's hand, and with a whisper said, "As they should be."

***

Laying down his load, Adam, drawing a handkerchief from his top pocket, mopped his brow as he walked toward the water bucket. His limp had gotten significantly better; and though Aretina had likely saved his leg, he knew his every step until his last would be a reminder of the road he'd traveled—with this he was content, and even grateful.

Having taken his fill of refreshment, he wet his hands to cleanse them of his daily toil, and then took up a pail on which to sit. Dropping with the grunt of one whose labors have been faithful and full, he extracted from his pocket the now tattered and well-used map; and, as he had every day since arriving, he read.

Some time into his study, a cool breeze brushed past his ankles, carrying with it a fallen leaf. The chill of the coming season was a welcome respite from the days of heat; it rushed over his body like the water of a crystal pool consuming a diver. And as he came alive once more, shaking off the last of the summer sun and day-end fatigue, he looked to the hills rising just above the fields of gold; and there he saw a woman in a silken dress, standing barefooted in the sweeping breeze coming o'er the plains and crashing against the hill like waves on a mighty rock. The ends of that vibrant, autumn-colored dress, like the ends of the sun-kissed forest falling over her shoulders in long, silken strands, danced as one with the wind; and the brilliance of the setting sun made her the evening star.

Rising from his pail, Adam drew in deeply the aromatic air rushing down from where she stood, while his eyes sealed tightly to better know the essence of that which overflowed within him. And, just as this rush of life had reached its peak, Adam unveiled his eyes for one last look to the hills, then turned and made a mad, limping sprint for the house, there to find Liam.

***

She stood alone on a hilltop, watching the summer fade into memory. The bitterness of winter lay just over the horizon, but there would be warmth enough to stay its mighty jaws. And as the day's final glow burst forth in white, and the cold air of the west descended upon her, she felt the touch of something coarse and rough brush gently against her palm and coil tenderly about her fingers. Her eyes sealed for but a moment as she returned a squeeze of her own, before opening them once more and into a world washed in white.

Chapter 6
Reality

*H*er eyes did flutter as the intensity of the white filled them, and it would be some time before she could fully regain the scene in which she helplessly turned.

Pale outlines were observed; curiously familiar shapes where presented; and through a pounding skull rippled a parade of frigid waves, scraping the roots of her hair as they crested, and slamming with tremendous force into a rather perplexed clump of grey matter.

Eventually, the bizarre shapes before her began slowly to converge upon her nose. And as her eyes disentangled themselves from one another, there emerged a blurry image of a silvery slab set beside a black rectangle, both painted against the side of a giant grey box.

"Miss?"

Her eyes focused some more.

"Miss? Can you hear me?"

Further focusing made a partially opened door of the silvery slab, a shadowy hallway of the black rectangle, and of the grey box some sort of room.

"Miss Adeline? Can you—*whoa!*"

Just as her muscles had commenced contracting in such a manner as to alter her present position into one offering a vantage point with a more favorable altitude, two soft forces acted upon her chest, forbidding any further progress.

"Don't sit up just yet, dear!" said the voice. "You've had a pretty nasty collision—could be concussed."

Tilting her head carefully back and to the left, Adeline beheld the school nurse kneeling beside her, wrapping in a towel a fresh ice pack.

"Standing in front of doors," the nurse mumbled with a shaking head as she worked, setting a thawed icepack beside a cooler of fresh ones. "Don't they teach sense in schools? Certainly, they don't teach chivalry. You know that boy?" she continued, now addressing Adeline. "The one in here with you—why, he bolted with a huff not two seconds after you hit the floor. Couldn't be bothered to help a lady! All he says is, 'She's *your* problem!'" Thusly spoke the nurse, dropping low her voice and performing some obnoxious mimicry. "Can you believe *that*? To be fair, it *had* been I who'd opened the door. But, in my defense, one does not expect to find students leaning against doors—who leans against doors, anyway?" Her speech was quickly becoming something like a nervous prattle. "Besides *you*, of course—and *why*? I mean, maybe I should be suing *you*—after all, you *did* give me quite a scare! I'm sure the beats my heart just skipped will come back to haunt me in the long run. This poor, old heart will try to catch up with itself, you know? And, like a dancer trying to make up for missed steps, it will try to force two—or even three!—missed beats into one! I could have a heart attack! Maybe I have already had one! Look at my face—is it blue? I feel blue. I can tell; I *must* be blue! Look at my hands! They're puffy! Oh, no! The stress is causing weight gain! These pants—I can feel the button about to burst! *You* did this! It was *YOU*! Standing in front of doors! Oh, cruel fate! How like fortune's fool am I! You'll probably *die* from this head trauma, and then you'll sue me! WELL, NOT TODAY, SISTER!" she screamed, slamming the fresh ice pack against Adeline's forehead with a *KNOCK*, which sounded very much like knuckles against wood, or a two-by-four batting a coconut—satisfying and nearly flawless in sound, though nonetheless painful. "I'm gonna keep you alive so I can sue *you* for attempted self-concussing in the first degree, premeditated to inflict undue emotional and cardiopulmonary distress upon an innocent door-opener! Don't think I won't! I know how Legal Magic works! I've seen Lawyer Magicians on television! I'll sue you for unwarranted stress-causing! I'll sue you for the malicious melting of my ice pack! I'll sue you for forcibly enlisting my labor! I'm a school nurse, not an on-call care provider! Get me a lawyer! Get me a judge and a jury and a hand slapper!"

These last remarks met Adeline's ears as fading echoes; amid bellowing the words "care provider," the nurse had leapt to her feet, sprinted through the door and down the hall, arms flailing wildly, and screaming at the tippy-top of her lungs at whomever her freewheeling, whipping, and waving hands happened to strike along the way, declaring that she'd sue them too, citing failure to provide a clearly disquieted woman the necessary space to express her internal calamity.

Sitting upright, Adeline found herself alone in the empty, quiet office.

Just beyond her position, she saw the two armchairs in which she and Adam had been sitting before what she now remembered was an abrupt meeting with the door.

Sucking her lips into her mouth and biting down on them, she let out a tearful sigh.

So, there had been no grand story after all: no disagreeable encounters with M.O.S.Q.U.I.T.O.E.S., no dabbling in Beauty Magic; no stopping Time, no singing in the lunchroom.

And there had been no Curse.

It had all been an unconscious hallucination.

This was, perhaps, even more so than the tragic failure she had dreamed, the most disappointing reality of her story.

Rising from the floor, Adeline collected the thawed and frozen icepacks, tossed them in the cooler, then placed it, as well as the towels in which the icepacks had been wrapped, upon the nurse's desk, before walking straight to the main office and promptly withdrawing herself from Enderbrine's. In reality, the process was not quite as smooth as might be conveyed by its facts being stuffed neatly into and related with the brevity of a single sentence. In her mind, however, it had indeed been this simple; all the coddling and coaxing turned to pressing and insisting, which soon became furious dictating and insulting, concluding at last in a disgusted dismissal—all this had passed as a single span of inconsequential time, bearing indistinguishable sounds, swirling about in a cloud of indifference and apathy, and laden with tremendous exhaustion.

In accordance with school policy, Adeline's records were burned, her progress turned to ashes, and on her forehead was stamped the mark of all Enders who, for whatever reason, had followed the same path as she now traveled. She'd seen students of the class she had now joined being escorted off the premises; stamps on their heads usually read "Dropout," but she had seen some particularly rebellious students wearing labels such as "Ignorant," "Moron," and "Loser." She cared not to know what hers read.

Forehead inked and skin blackened from having a pile of ashes tossed in her face, a dazed and dead-eyed Adeline was taken roughly by the arm and dragged out of the building. Just before said appendage had gone completely numb, she was cast into a puddle of mud just outside Enderbrine's gate, where hunched a hunchbacked grounds keeper, holding a hose and a bucket of something that looked like dirt—indeed, if there was any satisfaction to be had in this whole ordeal, it was that now Adeline had at last been given the answer as to why this persistent puddle of mud persistently existed, and how it had never dried nor become any less prominent.

Beneath the revolted gaze of the grounds keeper, there in the shadow of his long, upturned snout, she rose to her feet and, without bothering to brush herself off, set a course for somewhere, anywhere.

It didn't matter where.

Anywhere but here.

Chapter 7
Love

And, so, dear reader, we have come at last to the end; and here, as the tale draws near to its close, as the stagehands prepare to ring down the curtain on our titular players and their respective journeys, I must confess that there may have been an error in my reporting, made rather early in our acquaintance—at the very beginning, in fact: Chapter One, Paragraph Three, to be exact—when I had stated that in this tale there could be found no happy ending.

How did we get here? It's so strange; I just don't know what to make of it. As if another pen had emerged amid this tale's composition to make its mark upon the page, it appears the ending that this story's beginning had in etchings made by a pen of old ensured has been irrevocably altered; new lines gliding o'er the page do lead toward something quite the opposite of what had seemed inevitable, turning backward, even, the course of storytelling that ever treks from beginning to end.

I am a flawed Omniscient. Though I do attempt to meet the trying demands of this profession, to *know* all is far trickier a business than to *see* all. In my profession, one's all-seeing nature is confined to that upon which one is reporting—a grand scope, to be sure; but limited, nonetheless. And in this scope, what knowledge I am to relate is gathered through a great deal of study; sometimes, I even interview characters to gain further insight.

As with every one of Conners' pieces to which I am assigned, and in which I fully immerse myself that my omniscience might be as genuine as humanly possible, I conducted more research than what would be expected of an average omniscient narrator; thorough to a fault am I. Yet, in the process of piecing together this tale, I discovered just how foolishly titled is my practice—to have limits is to be disqualified from the realm of omniscience. And these limits were discovered when, in preparing this story's conclusion, my eyes were opened to the fact that, all this time, I had been blinded by my own understanding, my own interpretation.

For what of the heart know I?

What of the hands that, like a carpenter's, move against the block of wood can I discover?

What makes them to move?

What purpose drives them?

What vision employs them?

And by what name can they be called?

I said in the beginning that in this tale no happy ending could be found, for such a result would require a happy outcome for all parties upon whom the story focuses. If happiness had come to one party, but not the other, my conscience would not allow any phrases like "happily ever after" to fall upon the page (unless done so, as here, in the form of an example).

True it is, as you will see, that there is for but one a well-established manifestation of bliss by the time the last word falls; however, what my limits, roadblocks of my own making, had prevented me from grasping is the fact that here, in this final chapter, will one story indeed come to an end; but from this end there rises a chance for a new beginning. And if that chance is taken, if a new beginning—as with the one you and I, dear reader, have already experienced together: the very one that had changed my entire perspective—is discovered in the rubble,

then what would have been a tragic ending becomes the doorway to a happy beginning, one without an end. But that will be
for the final pages to tell, and for those written long before the
bones were formed to be fulfilled.

And, so, I will bid you now adieu, and release you into the
final chapter of the tale already written, there to see for yourself
how unlike the ends of old the final turning of the page could
be.

***

It would be many years before the events related in the pile of
pages preceding this one would come alive again in the mind of
our leading lady.

Long, indeed, did she wander.

Traveling this way and that, Adeline had sought respite, but
had sacrificed what rest she'd known for endless waking toil. By
most accounts, the pieces of her life had finally fallen into place.
The earth was green and fruitful, skies were bright and blue;
an ever-rising sun did she know, but its fire was forgotten. For
those who came to know her face and know it well, words like
Beauty and Poise, meaningless as they had been, were discarded
and replaced altogether; renamed were these carnal phenome-
na, renamed after she who was now the personification thereof.
Like the marble of an idol standing aloft in a courtyard of flour-
ishing colors did she become: shaped to perfection, elegant,
desired, and impervious (at least, in the moment that was her
present day) to all the ails of life that tormented those who wor-
shiped in her garden. In robes like meadows sprouting precious
gems and stones was she adorned. Her tongue knew naught

but the sweetest wine and her stomach only the heartiest, most wholesome foods. Her palace was far grander than surely even the halls of a goddess, and in it she could scarce contain the entirety of her wealth.

Long, indeed, did she wander.

She had searched for comfort, but forfeited what warmth she'd possessed for a heart of ice and a bed of stone; she'd hunted knowledge, but tore at wisdom with rabid teeth and set aflame that which her feelings forbade. Confused lines and endless circles had been her paths; without purpose, she stumbled about; without direction, she drifted, until she could hear naught but one adventure beckoning to her soul.

Adeline had seen what the eyes of the world craved; she understood their longing, for it was the very same longing inside of her. And, dressing in the ever-changing gowns of Desire and Adoration, she, for a great many years, offered herself as the lifeblood by which beat the hearts of those who did in flame sacrifice daily upon her altar their very selves and the fleeting sands that tumbled—unmarked, unused, and unsung—through their hourglass. But even having become a master wielder of a multitude of Magic, Adeline could find no water to quench her own thirst. Admiration, idolization, wealth, fame, and power: these did she possess, and possess in spades; yet, they were hollow nothings, phantom forms slipping through her fingers like dust and ashes, like vapor, like smoke.

It was in this time, somewhere along the hazy void of emptiness, that she happened upon a package. Not one to rummage through fan mail, a night of intoxication at the studio had ended with her having deemed the dumpster behind the building a fit place in which to sleep off another successful session. And when the sun arose that morning, peeling back the lids of her bloodshot eyes, Adeline found herself sprawled over not only a week's worth of refuse, but also bags of mail from her devoted followers.

Removing a slimy piece of uneaten lettuce from her head, and peeling a long hair of something from the corner of her mouth, Adeline grabbed a bag of discarded fan mail, propped herself up against the side of the dumpster, and began to dig.

There was no shortage of manic obsession, worship, and adulation; not one of these well-represented types was in any way unique from the last or the next. There were obscene pieces, as well as those containing depraved animosity, and even violent threats. She was immune to it all. Even the sincere letters, offering thanks for how her existence had been and was a light in darkness, fell bitterly against her heart, as poison on the tongue; for she knew better what she was than did those whose lives had by the mask she wore been changed. So many prayers, all lifted in her name—all unheeded; all unanswered.

On and on she dug through these bags of unread and unwanted offerings to her alter, indifferent to it all, but uninspired to lift herself from the dumpster and explore idleness elsewhere.

And then her hands fell upon a package.

Here and there along the way she had given a glance to the markings of envelopes, packages, and boxes, but to them paid little mind. This package's markings, however, leapt off the paper and smacked her squarely between the eyes.

In the middle had been written her name, right above the address to the very dumpster in which she sat. But in the upper corner was writ a name of old: Adam.

For a great long while she stared at this name. And, to be

sure, 'twas Adam's—indeed, the very same!

All at once, a flash flood of all the emotions she had once known to be associated with that name rushed through her; and though there was pain to be remembered, it was the innocence she perceived at the root of it all that spurred her to hope as once she did—as a schoolgirl, as a naïve woman-in-the-making—to hope that *this* could indeed be something.

What was that something?

Who could tell?

And how ridiculous!

How absurd!

After all these years, there could be nothing left from the past to plant in what had been the garden of the future a seed now to blossom!

That ship had sailed!

Or...had it?

Adeline pondered every angle of the matter, including those scenarios in which Adam sought to dip his toes into her fortune, or to seduce her emotions that he might wear her as a badge of boasting before his buddies. By the end of all this pondering, she could think of no honorable reason Adam could have had to have made contact—save, of course, for the laughable notion that he was strung out on love, desperate to see her once more, to wash her feet with aromatic tears of sorrow, and like a dog pledge his love and loyalty to her and her alone, for as long as they both should live.

Ridiculous.

Adeline took a moment to let the goosebumps of the idea subside.

No—it was a stupid notion.

Adam didn't love her.

He never had.

There could be no good reason for him to have made contact.

He was a rat when she knew him, and a rat was he still today.

She had lost more than enough sleep, dried enough tears, to even consider…

Wait a minute—now, *there's* an idea!

Yes!

A perfect revenge!

Package in hand, Adeline leapt from the dumpster and made a beeline into her studio, where she set in motion the most elaborate and thorough ornamenting: she showered away the grime and bathed in sweet-smelling oils, lathered her skin in lotions, wrapped her body in the finest and most elegant robes, tied her hair into an intricate design, and decorated her ears, neck, and fingers with her most expensive and most dazzling diamonds, while in her head there played a vision of a desperate, dying man kneeling in the blistering sand, his tongue panting for a drink; and on that tongue she'd place a drop from a tall bottle of ice-cold refreshment, before casting it all into the sand to be consumed by the sun.

Adeline would have told you that she had seen the world, that her work had taken her everywhere worth seeing. This address, however, the one on the package—this one would have made her a liar.

Her plane had touched down just before the afternoon. Following several hours of driving in a direction being increasingly swallowed by silence and devoured by isolation, her horizon was at last so filled with a grand and wonderful spectacle that she could not bear one more moment seeing it whiz past her unappreciated.

Pulling her car along the side of the road, Adeline exited her steel machine and stood on the running board. Her eyes could not widen enough to drink in all they so desired to taste; and when at last they had swallowed so much that some began to overflow in the form of crystal tears, she veiled her eyes, and, raising high her arms, turned her head to the heavens that she might absorb the majesty of a place in which the beauty of nature knew no bounds, nor any hands by which to be scarred.

Leaving gladly her busy and congested world behind for one of bright and brilliant colors bursting forth from the bosom of the earth, Adeline grabbed from her car the yet unopened package and promptly set for the remainder of the journey a walking course.

Crossing the dirt road toward the untamed, untouched world of miracles that was exploding in blissful brilliance beside it, Adeline reached a threshold of green. Stepping immediately out of her shoes, she let her naked feet sink deeply into the soft and welcoming bed before her; and as she walked that day, over hills dressed like a forest canopy, sprinkled with the colors of sunshine and sunsets, through virescent woods and rows upon rows of trees casting purple confetti into the breeze and filling the air with the aroma of paradise—as she walked through this glorious land, she shed, little by little, the diamonds and jewels from her fingers, ears, and around her neck; her hair was liberated to be entwined with the wind; makeup was wiped away that she might better know the kiss of the sunshine and the tender brush of the wind; her fancy clothes were crudely but happily

modified into a makeshift t-shirt and breezy skirt; the sweat running over her brow and rising through her pores was a welcome
washing of her oiled skin, while dirt and mud and grime showered her with nature's cleansing intimacy; and with every gulp of
the free and clean air, she saw in her mind an image of herself
taking the place of the desperate, dying man kneeling in the
blistering sand, panting for a drop of water.

About the time the sun had come to rest upon a bed of treetops, Adeline, having long forgotten what reason had brought
her to this place, came upon a hill of green. More alive than
ever she had been, Adeline took the hill at a sprint; and when
the final step of the climb had fallen upon the earth, she sprang
forth gaily into the air, then floated down like a feather to the
soft bed below.

When at last she had caught her breath from the boister-
ous laughter and joyous pain, she rolled onto her stomach and
scanned the next chapter of her journey through this never-end-
ing phenomenon; and there below she saw a field of gold.

Far more dazzling in color than any piece of jewelry she'd
ever owned, far more lovely than any arrangement she'd ever
draped over her flesh, far more rich than any viand on which
she'd ever fed, far more bounteous than all her worldly wealth,
and far more alive than ever she could hope to be was this extraordinary field. How it swayed in the evening breeze; how
with the wind it lifted a wondrous song she longed to know;
how it glowed like the sun in which it bathed, and put to shame
the sunny locks that had been such an item of perfection in the
eyes of her masses; how humbling it was, this field, like all she
had seen; yet, it was here the feeling, the true understanding, hit
her in so paralyzing a fashion that even when her eyes took note

of human activity just beyond the swaying gold, she had not the strength for yet a while longer to stand.

With her belly still to the earth, and her head propped up on her hands, she watched as the human commotion grew to feature more than one individual.

It began with a child, skipping and leaping about, breathing only giggles, with his arms raised high and grasping wildly at the air, as if after a butterfly. Long did she admire the lad, bouncing about in the green pasture between the apple-red barn and the picturesque house whence he'd emerged, all the while wondering if ever she had been so lost in simple euphoria. Soon after waddled into the scene a second child, much younger, appearing to have only recently found her legs; and right behind her was a most handsome woman, dressed in a long and wind-tossed gown of sun-bleached red, her umber locks playing in the breeze, while her voice of a summer song called after the little ones to be near. And then, as the warmth of this scene, taken straight from the pages of a storybook, seemed to have reached its peak, there came a shriek of unrestrained excitement from the lips of the children, as into the green pasture limped a man.

Shedding his plow and tying his horse to the fence, he tossed his hat high into the air and fell to his knees with arms stretched wide; and, catching the running children in his embrace, he bellowed a cry of laughter, as one who is after many painfully long years at last reunited with those he adores.

Her heart now a puddle in her chest, Adeline watched as the man rose to greet the woman, wrapping her tightly in his arms and pressing his lips to hers. They seemed to desire nothing more than to remain for the rest of time enveloped by and within the other; and Adeline felt a twinge of hunger to know something so desperately passionate and thoroughly pure.

The sun began to sink below the treetops, and the woman took the children by their hands and led them into the house, while the man returned to his horse and untied it from the fence. It was then Adeline found the strength to stand, for as the man released the reins and turned toward the barn, his face was made clear and completely unobstructed by the picturesque scene in which it was framed.

Adam.

Behind that crooked nose, somewhere under the scars on his face, there in that broken body, limping along the footpath, was indeed the boy she'd known once and long ago.

There were no dots to connect and interpret, no doubts with which to wrestle.

It was he.

Sure as the setting sun, it was he.

It was Adam.

Though he labored through the tiredness of the day, made all the more strenuous by a well- and long-known, incurable damage, not once did his smile recede or lose even a glint of its luster. But on the face of she who watched him go, there was naught but grief, washed in a downpour of guilt and sadness; for in this man were found her words: Beauty undone, a face marred, stiffness nested in grace; tormented flesh, broken and twisted—and how many more like these might he have known!

Falling to her knees, Adeline wept, as the words of her Curse, uttered in a dream so many years ago, crashed about in her mind like restless waves on an ocean of black. What Magic was this, thought she, that could take from dreams words of hurt and hatred, and spin the desires thereof into a thorn of suffering?

Surely, it had all been a dream!

Those words she had never spoken; though, in the silence of her heart were they screamed through tears of rage. How could the wicked wishes of the heart be made reality without action? Oh, cruel Magic, to bring crashing down upon him against whom she had become inflamed to wield the lash, yet had never raised a hand! What fiendish sorcery to heed the utterings of the heart and ignore the silence of the lips! Was Magic so unfeeling that it would form deed from desire, disregarding conscious restraint?

And yet, here it was: the product of her wishes past!

Might it now be too late to undo what she had done?

Weak and weary, there on her knees in the red glow of the sunset, Adeline raised her fists to the sky and spoke into the wind from both heart and mouth, "My dearest Adam—forgive me! Desperately undone by the wretched desires of my heart! I release thee! By all that I am, I release thee! Be free at last, and forevermore—be free from the clutches of my wicked Curse!"

A great gust of wind, warm and filled with the aroma of all that was beautiful, now draped thinly in shadow, rushed about her, catching up the ends of her hair and lifting her from the lush green of the hill, before her outstretched arms and body fell, heavy with exhaustion, to the ground, where she came to rest with her face buried in the package she had yet to open. Rising slowly to her knees once more, she took it in hand, and then glanced o'er the fields of gold. There was Adam, resting his arms atop the fence and surveying the precious here and now, before pulling a book from his back pocket, oblivious to the hill above him. In his profile, Adeline could see that his smile yet persisted, there beneath a still crooked nose, beside a scarred face, and above a stiffness that he rubbed intermittently as he read.

Perhaps, thought she, there had been no Magic after all, no Curse sent forth to maim this man's life and make his world undone, for he was just as he had been before she'd released him: his flesh was yet broken and twisted, lacking grace, and holding but a faded memory of his former self, as per the once cruel desire of her heart; though she saw no grand towers or sparkling jewels, she beheld immeasurable wealth; she saw no grand mansion, yet a home there was, set above a fruitful earth, beside nature's finest gold, and beneath crystal skies.

His was a world quite the opposite of undone, and so did it appear to have been long before her lifting a cry of release.

Retracting her gaze, Adeline's hands gripped the package; and, with a sharp inhale, she began to tear.

Inside she found a strip of dark blue leather, atop of which sat a white slip of paper, whereupon had been writ a brief message.

Dear Adeline,

This had been a gift from an old friend of mine. I had never known how wayward my paths had been until this map made them clear and gave me a new path on which to tread. Read it well, and keep your eyes ahead.

Until we meet again,
Adam

Adeline's eyes had just finished tracing the final curve of the last letter in the name of the note's composer, when yet another great gust of wind snatched the paper from her weakening hand and carried it swiftly into the distance.

***

The day offered little now by which to continue his reading. So, tucking back into his pocket the book he had inherited from Liam, Adam heaved an abundantly contented sign, and turned to retire for the evening. As he did so, his foot fell upon what he perceived to be a rather noisy leaf—too noisy, however, for *this* time of year.

Looking down, he took from the dirt a slip of paper that, when his eyes had at last adjusted to the quickly darkening world closing in about him, infected him with a great start. Those same eyes immediately began to dart this way and that, left and right, and then upward to the hill, where he could have sworn he saw a shadow deeper than the rest slip away quickly into the darkness.

A name wrapped in a billow of air rocketed from deep within his belly, shooting straight and true through his throat, ready to be cast forth into the final winks of the day.

But this call he stopped.

The name he swallowed.

And, clutching tightly in his fist and raising slowly to his lips the letter he'd penned, Adam, as a tear ran the length of his cheek, cast forth a smile to the hill, and then limped back to the house, there to rejoin his family at the head of his table.

***

She knew not where she was when the morning rays tenderly

lifted the lids of her eyes the next morning; it had been a blind run through the dark of night, halted only when exhaustion had at last taken hold and sent her dropping mid-stride into the bosom of the meadow.

Rising slowly, she surveyed the newness of the day. She would have been content to sit for the rest of her life there in the soft bed she had enjoyed all through the night; but she knew she had to find her feet, to move on, to leave this world behind in the hope that the mess she'd made might be with her removed.

It was time, now, to let it be, and be without her.

Moving to stand, she threw a hand into the ground, and in so doing slammed her palm directly into the package. She had lost all track of it during the night; there existed no memory of her having clutched it as she ran. Yet, here it was, opened by only a tear, the dark blue leather contents staring back at her.

Though she felt it would make little difference, she could not deny that the dose of curiosity the sight of the package had and did feed was rather potent; plus, there existed a twinge of guilt for carrying out a permanent departure without first (or, last) giving an old friend's gift the proper consideration.

Sitting back down, Adeline took the package in hand and tore it. Onto her lap fell a tattered book, bound in dark blue leather; and on its face, worn nearly into being flush with the rest of that face, was an imprint: a symbol, one she recognized; yet, of which she knew little. It was a long vertical line, with a short, horizontal line pinned near the apex of the former: a cross. Examining further, she found this word imprinted into the spine: Bible.

She had seen many books of Magic in her day.

This was not one of them.

For when she peeled back the cover, she found nothing at all of Magic, but rather something far grander, something that would shatter the shaken faith, held now by but a thread, in that which had been fed to her since her youth.

There was no magic here.

The sun burned brilliantly overhead when at last she rose from the meadow. Though she had had no breakfast, she had feasted all through the morning. Stepping forth, with her nose pressed firmly against her map, Adeline's foot fell upon a soft and warm bed of rich soil; and on that path, faithfully, did she tread to wherever it would so lead.

The End

CLOSING LETTER
FROM WAYWARD PATHS

THE journey that is taking hold of a story, an idea, and escorting it onto the page from the mind, heart, and being, is a tale in itself. From my very earliest pieces, to my first composed (and yet unreleased) novel, and across every single scrap of paper on which the essence of my passion has bled in streaks of black, there is not one collection of pen-, pencil-, or keystrokes in want of its own sub-surface narrative.

Adam & Adeline's behind-the-scenes tale is among the more unique, standing very much on its own amid the titles comprising the emerging world of Connerian literary arrangements, as its composition fell in the midst of a most extraordinary change in my life—and, by extraordinary, I mean that something truly outside my ordinary took hold of the reins that had long borne the shredded flesh of my skin and crimson stains of my bloody struggle, transforming and fundamentally altering the backdrop that was the time of my writing this book, as well as the direction in which I was compelled to pen.

Never did I intend for *Adam & Adeline* to be anything other than a silly short story; more than that, I never at the time of its genesis could have conceived of the final product it would become. When I first sat down to interpret into words the spark of inspiration that was *Adam & Adeline*, I was toying with a preposterous idea centered around magic and star-crossed romance—something quick and easily digestible; something comic, almost cartoony, and able to snag a laugh or two; something to poke fun at fairy tales of old, and still maintain a twinge of heart to rend the emotional fortitude of the reader before the curtain fell. But on that day in 2015, a void of darkness drifted lazily over the page, obscuring the head-to-hand translation; not one more word could be related. Years later, this heap of broken pieces behind the pen would learn the reason why.

Almost ten years on the run was I when *Adam & Adeline* was begun, and not a mile far enough had I gone. Of the particulars, I shall not be exhaustive in my narration—but know this: Knowledge and Understanding were the kings of my longing; and from my earliest, I sought these distant masters by many avenues. Where the trail led, I ever knew not; upon which trail to tread was ever mine to choose. How many were my paths, and all broad enough to bind a blind and manic sprinter.

Far from the lanes and alleys to which pointed the unquestioning regurgitators of pre-digested information; far from the mind-molding mitts of modernity's many marionettes; far from fortified foundations forbidding the flame of query and examination; far from it all, and deep into mystery and wonder, did I venture, sinking headlong into a realm of curious challenging, testing that which I had by vicious blows upside the head from the club of contemporary classroom conditioning been well assured, lectured, and sternly instructed were unshakeable certainties, intolerable to be questioned. And among my numerous arenas of independent study was a topic likewise presented with the assertion of assurance: God.

In school, I found myself increasingly disinterested with the tasteless, nutrient-deprived morsels laid before me to be chewed only long enough that they might be vomited back up and onto

the test page. In church, I found myself increasingly disillu-
sioned, even bored, with the image of a divine Creator—a being
situated somewhere far away, high in the clouds—of whom I'd
heard and read much, but could never quite reach. Yet, where the
hours passed in the classroom sent me scouring the library for
more stimulating, nourishing bites to gnaw and digest, church
sent me diving into the Bible to see if anything akin to meat
could there be found.

Truly, as a youth, I was far more interested in Shakespeare,
astronomy, space travel, and world history—not to mention fri-
volity, and a great deal of idleness and goofing off—than I was
in God; but, as the years progressed, revelations of truth began
to grip my senses; and it wasn't long until I began to realize not
only that God exists, but also that my heart and I were wandering somewhere dangerously far from His presence.

Where libraries—as well as innumerable transfixed gazes into
unobstructed, night skies—revealed in the bounty and beauty
blooming from the arts and sciences, as well as in the depraved
savagery and inevitable destructions presented in human history, evidence of the very existence of God, the Bible gripped the
back of my head and forced me to examine my life, and there
see that, even though I was involved in a church, I was of the
body of Christ not a member. My distance haunted me; my
conscience hunted me; and try though I did to cross the chasm
between the evanescent and the eternal, I could build nothing
strong enough to bear my weight to the other side.

Quickly disintegrating beneath the weight of my helplessness, the enervation from my ardent striving, and the apparent
hopelessness of my cause—there, at the age of sixteen, standing in the midst of an empty sanctuary, my eyes boring deeply

and aflame into a towering, wooden cross, casting its shadow over me—I demanded God step forth and answer my cry. For I knew myself: as much as I wanted to do right, I simply never could; my sin was pervasive, adherent to my very being; and how wretched had I become, even in so short a time. After all I had done, tried to do, even with all my violent penitence, I knew neither peace nor security; only hauntings of my past and waking present—an infinite string of twisted evils, revealed anew every day—could be found to cool my starving tongue.

If God wanted me, let Him step forth and prove it.

But God responded not to my demand.

Such silence had been bestowed also upon the various means of *magical* manipulation I'd religiously lifted to tempt His favor: prayers, practices, and, as mentioned, perfervid penitence.

To these spells and incantations, He was unmoved.

There was no magic capable of saving the damned.

Still, even in this silence, it could not be concluded that He wasn't there.

Such would have been, at the very least, intellectually dishonest; and to be so was my abhorrence.

To scour the depths had been my practice in the pursuit of mystery; to harness my comprehensive capacity had been my eager aim when considering the infinite, the eternal, the unseen. But I had not gone far enough. Though I would have said otherwise, I had indeed overlooked something; and that something emerged onto the scene, and in so sub-microscopic a manifestation, when, face to the floor, exhausted, there in that empty sanctuary, I pondered the question: Does God even want me?

With election and other doctrines of predestination was I familiar. Perhaps, thought I, my name was never meant to be in

His book.

That's when faith began. For even if He truly didn't want me, I desperately needed Him.

There was at this time no great understanding of the face of God, nor, even, of Christ and the Gospel. Still, though simple in my comprehension thereof, I truly believed the Word: that Jesus is the Son of God, who died in the place of sinners and was raised from the dead, enduring the wrath of God in our place, satisfying it as never we could, so that all who believe in Him would be justified as sinless before the judgment seat of the Father, and be called children of God. And, so, onto this I clamped my talons, declaring that I could stand upon nothing else, and in so doing let loose the leashes affixed to my countless, mad attempts, all thrashing and pulling in every direction like feral beasts, each with a mind to seek and devour the prize of salvation. I chose to believe what the Bible says of God, rather than what my heart had been interpreting of Him from the absence of a spiritual experience.

I had been seeking something magical.

What I needed was something relational.

And, so, my feet were set upon the narrow way. But the world is a cunning huntress; and even before I had breached the waters of baptism, this deserter of the temporal realm was placed in the crosshairs.

Now, what has all this to do with *Adam & Adeline*? With my conversion nearly ten years in my wake, my life was careening toward ultimate destruction. The cunning huntress had employed no clever tricks against this lone, enfeebled youth; being ever isolated in my pursuits for understanding, I was an easy target for deception—blunt, was I, with neither a faith nor an intellect sharp enough to cut through the veil of treachery being cast over me, nor with strength enough to clasp the mightiest of swords, resting at my fingertips. But of these things I never explicitly wrote (though, one cannot but identify the lack of happy endings and general aura of hopelessness in much of my work up to this point). And I had no intention, this time, of writing anything of the kind when I first penned the words, "Adam and Adeline."

As it turned out, I didn't really write anything at all.

Rather unconsciously—or, so it seems to me now—I merely placed upon the page the words of a piece already composed. But this I did not see until long after the book had been completed.

When I again took up the pen, three years after laying it down, and with no shortage of darkness passing there between, I slowly began developing a plot that, in my mind, had no distinct direction, story arc, or real conclusion. I was writing blindly, but there was a tremendous motivation I could not explain that kept propelling me forward; the words were made known to me only as they were formed upon the page.

All along the way, elements of a life past would manifest themselves as integral stitches in the grand tapestry; and—markedly, consciously, even willingly—I permitted them be woven into the design. How like whispers they were, these elements, for such had they become in my life; yet, and very much in contrast to my complexion, I could not forbid them. Indeed, I welcomed them.

What I could not see then I see now, ever so vividly.

In writing *Adam & Adeline*, I was inadvertently—though, not by accident—revealing to myself, and now to my readers, where my paths had led when I'd set my eyes beyond the Father's house.

The first four chapters were a vent for my potent frustrations founded upon the youth I had squandered, my bitterness toward the worthless "education" that had swallowed the majority of my life and left me at its culmination with empty pockets, no job, and a most expensive piece of paper, fit only to collect dust on the wall. It was an outlet for the dissatisfaction, disillusionment, and distain I had reaped from my time sowing to the winds of the world; and I drove hard to the core of the issue: the depraved and deceitful heart of man.

With love for all mankind, but ever hostile toward the fundamentals of humanism (in that man is basically, or born, good), I raged against the prevailing deification of the heart; for if there was one belief corresponding to Biblical truths I had not cast aside along the seemingly endless, winding, and rocky paths, down which I had forfeited much in the quest to lighten my burden, only to find my back breaking beneath a mighty weight, my feet blistering with each ponderous pace—if there was one thing I had not relegated to the miry ravines, it was this understanding, this belief, and this increasingly self-evident certainty that the heart is deceitful and desperately wicked. And this point was hard-ridden throughout the first four chapters, the effects of allegiance to the every beat of the heart painting in the blood of its treachery the events therein, until at last being related in explicit detail the moment Adeline discovers the black book in her cellar.

What had been a release of tremendous frustration was after

the conclusion of the book revealed unto me to be a retelling of my first steps toward the pig sty.

Upon my conversion, I went seeking a deepening of my relationship with Christ, only to very quickly be swallowed up into a carnival Christianity, masquerading as highly spiritual. Faith was traded for fun—such even became the indicator of the sincerity of one's connection to God; reverence was traded for revelry, holiness for hedonism, and Christ for a chasm. So adrift had I become upon this ferry to hell, painted in hues of living color, that for a great long while I lost all reason; only sensation remained. And, so, my days grew terribly dark.

Not unlike Adeline, when the feelings began to fall short, when the fun began to fizzle out, I sprang right into action, resolved to discern, decipher, and, if necessary and possible, divine the proper process of reestablishing my connection to God.

But I had completely forgotten my way home.

Not two years since clinging to the cross in faith, I had hurled myself right back into the pit, wherein could be found naught but pervasive despondency. So, like Adeline, when all the books and sermons and sayings and beatings of my tormented spirit had in my hands turned up empty, when all that I had been painstakingly building by my own council began to crumble all around me, I furiously purged my life of all things related to God and filled my eyes with the mad desires of my heart, until they bled in black streaks over my existence.

All of this had taken place six years prior to *Adam & Adeline*'s conception, during which I supped on and studied skepticism and avidly adopted agnosticism; the repercussions of this time had become my identity—though, very much like an object held in one's vision for an extended period of time, I could not truly see what I had become. So much time focused on myself, I was no longer flesh and blood, but rather a lens through which to see the world, oblivious to the distortions of my very being. Thus, at the time of writing, I could not recognize just how similar Adeline's path was to my own. But the most potent punches in this inadvertent allegorical autobiography of sorts came as I sat down to pen Chapter 5.

Longest of the seven, Chapter 5, in accordance with the overall compositional theme, was not at all planned out when the first stroke fell; it just sort of happened. In this chapter, Adam's choices finally catch up to him, and he is left with nothing but an empty cell and seven days of confinement. After my own slew of such choices, I, aged twenty-two, collapsed into my own, internal confinement, there to dwell, shivering in fear, as the world passed me by—seven years of paralyzing fear, to which I desperately clung as it shattered my mind and stripped me of what remnants of family, friends, and a life had not yet been taken by the fire.

From this pit of darkness, I thought I'd never escape.

But, all the while, God would not leave me.

Though He did allow this breakdown and self-imprisonment, He was ever at my door, offering me the sustenance I needed to revive, as did Bear for Adam. But, like Adam, I rejected His kindness every time. The mere thought of Him revolted me—a reaction very much akin to sticking one's own finger down one's throat. I raged at Him to leave me be—how much I wanted to die, to summon the courage to raise my hand, to pass through cowardly hesitation and grasp action, and so be free of Him and this noisome existence.

But He remained.

Upon Adam's release from prison, he is set upon a path; and how he walks did tell the tale of how I'd wandered after my conversion. To comforts, bright lights, and fun he is drawn from a path that is becoming increasingly uncertain, as he has neglected to examine the map he's been given. With no regard for that same map, I, too, was easily diverted from the narrow way and into the house of worldly pleasure. And, there, I relished in revelry that affixed itself to my soul like a cancer cell. Memories of those days are painted in shades of veiled midnight.

Though I had no connection at the time to this particular memory, it came to me some while later that the scene in which Adam enters Dolores' room captures the very same sensation I had felt when I nearly gave myself to a woman I hardly knew.

Twenty years old at the time, I was taken by the hand to her bedroom; I can still hear the creaking of the stairs echoing through the halls of the dark and empty house. Her room was dimly lighted in hues of red; as I entered, the floor began to creep slowly up the nearby wall, and with each step forward my head would swell, painfully, even to the point of compromising my vision—a dizzy, streaky, hazy mess filled my eyes; yet, I can still perceive with perfect clarity the rose-hued room and she standing in its midst. As her soft words tumbled lazily to my ears, I could acutely feel a great pressure acting against my chest—so powerful was this force that I could hardly draw breath. Then, as if the walls of the house had suddenly crumbled, permitting swift, broad passage to the vortex of frigid winter swirling violently without, a sense of cold dread consumed me.

I had to get out of there.

I ran and never looked back.

This memory, as stated, was not recalled as I wrote Adam's encounter with Dolores. What did fill me, however, was a Bible verse: Proverbs 5:5. Speaking of the "forbidden woman," the verse reads, "Her feet go down to death;" and so stark was this in my mind, so pressing upon my very being, so necessary and relevant to truly capture this scene I was discovering, that there freely and simply flowed from my hands the moment Adam regards the tattoos on Dolores' feet: one of the horse, made pale by her skin (and, thus, like one of Revelation's four horsemen), in whose body are found the letters "A" and "D;" and the other of the skull, the teeth of which bear the Latin word *mortem*—*Ad Mortem*: Unto Death.

Like Adam's realization in this moment that he is no longer wearing his backpack, in which is contained the map, so too did I feel exposed and vulnerable the night God turned me out of this forbidden woman's room.

But Adam and I would not so quickly turn back to the path; indeed, we proceeded to flip the map upside down, that it might more favorably fit our chosen course. In embracing the world, we both found a blink of bliss before becoming desolate. What once seemed friendly became hostile; where there had been bounty was now barrenness; and, having been devoured by the world, we came out the other side reviled. And it was here, at the peak of my insanity, amid the ruin my life had hastily become, that I was at last broken.

My life was in an uproar; it was falling to pieces behind the scenes of my best projection of dignity. But I was indeed a naked, noisome, vile beast, crawling about on my stomach, feeding on dirt and refuse; and there above me loomed the world, ready to deliver the final blow.

On the verge of utter ruin, I sped down a darkened road, every horrible choice from a brief lifetime relishing in vanity and pursuits of pleasure hard on my heels, snapping like the coming winter streaming through my opened windows. And I screamed again to the heavens, just as I had in the empty sanctuary twelve years prior, unsure if I would again find silence to answer me, not knowing if I was betraying my reason to hope in anguish and desperation that there is a power beyond myself that could catch this hand as it sunk beneath the waves of my existence. For I had so forgotten the way home that I could scarce even recall the image of Him who waited there for me. Enraged and afraid, feeling confounded at every turn, with every pursuit to elevate me even just to my feet crumbling to dust, I let out a feral roar, admitting my helplessness and telling God that I was done trying, that I had wandered down wayward paths to pig stys far from the house in which I had once known the love of His embrace, and that I was something the word "sorry" had no power whatsoever to convey.

There was in me no capacity to crawl back to Him, or to stay the crushing blow in the offing; but I swore that night that no matter what happened, I would forever be His servant, if He would but take command of my life and do with it as He pleased—it had never been mine, anyway; and it was worthless in my hands.

And, while I was still a long way off, He ran to me.

He ran.

***

Friend, I come not to you with a message saying that Christ is the means to your ends, or mine. Nor do I claim that He is the key to a life without trouble. Like Adam, I yet bear the scars and twisted features of years past; I yet carry the limp, the stiffness from my breaking. But I have Christ; I have the map; and, ever since my return from wayward paths, I have finally come to see what my attempts in the vein of religious striving (what I have hitherto dubbed "magic") had proved impotent to produce: the reality, beauty, and urgent necessity of Christ. Where sub-microscopic faith had moved my lips to declare that Jesus is Lord and my heart to believe that God raised Him from the dead, I have now an abundant assurance of salvation and a faith so radical that I care no longer for anything outside of His will. It truly is no longer I who live, but rather Christ who lives in me; for I have indeed forfeited all to His lordship—where He would have me go, so shall I go.

Free of my fear, liberated from my chains, healed and held upright, my labor is now for my Lord; and, by His grace, may it ever be. He who writes today is not the man who sat down to write all those years ago; and what an inconceivable impossibility this man would have been to the mind of Conners past. Where I go from here, I cannot say; once so keen on preserving and making the most of time, I realize now I never had any control over or claim to it; once devout to the fashioning of my own destiny, I defer to someone better qualified for such work. I cannot be anxious about the future, for it is not mine to write. I am not the man I was. And for that I can take no credit.

In light of all I have related, it may be asked why the text of *Adam & Adeline* is not a more explicitly Christian read—not once is the name of Christ mentioned. The reason is this, what I hope to have conveyed with this letter: I had no intention of making the story what it became, and by the time it was done I had not yet left the pig sty; my eyes had only just lifted from the mire. And it was my decision to preserve the tale as it was written, to not go back and retroactively transform it into something it wasn't at the time of its completion. What of it should be made explicit I hope to have conveyed properly and clearly in this letter.

And now, dear reader, my friends, my family: I step forth among you and declare that the Conners of old is dead, and life begins anew. I do very much appreciate your taking the time to attend to this letter. It is my sincere hope that you did enjoy the tale of *Adam & Adeline*, and that from it you have gleaned a blessing equal to the profound and all-encompassing joy I experienced whilst composing it. As stated previously, I know not what to expect of my work as the next steps fall. My narrator and I have been working diligently on a most extraordinary project; he and I are both very eager to get this project onto the shelves. (Bookstores and libraries have already been advised to reinforce their displays and bookcases with rebar and whatever else they deem necessary—if you'd thought my Ramblings were long and laborious, wait 'til you get a load of these puppies!). Wherever the new Connerian trail leads, I am at last assured that the way is true and the path is right.

I thank you again, with most hearty thanks, for reading. Fare thee well and may God's blessing be ever upon you.

Yours Very Sincerely,

C. K. Conners

Author Bio

C. K. Conners was born sometime, somewhere, and is still alive elsewhere. He is known by some as a hopeless romantic, a wearying wit, a formidably fluent fantasist, but most of all, *Who?*

When he's not writing about himself in the third person, this *what's-his-name* can be found flying in his private jet to exotic places, wine tasting with international business moguls, or philosophizing in robes and sandals on the steps of academia with fellow, curious-minded pupils—or, to put it more accurately, one can usually assume with confidence that on any given day Conners is locked in his room, wearing holey sweatpants and tattered moccasins, rocking a bedhead hairdo that would make Einstein jealous, sitting hunched over a blank piece of paper, and carving thereon the chicken scratch hieroglyphs he hopes to one day pass off as novels.

If he were, in any way, an interesting person, perhaps more than this could be relayed. But, alas, he is about as common as a scraped knee, and equally agreeable.

Route 27 Publishing

Founded in April 2018 by author C. K. Conners, Route 27 Publishing® and its children's books imprint Randy Boy Books® feature exclusively the literary madness produced by its founder, CEO, and bearer of basically every other company role. Though presently comparable in earnings to a not-for-profit organization, Route 27 Publishing® aims to one day grow large enough to employ full-time its founder, CEO, etcetera, etcetera, and bring into the public light all the tales he so desires to tell before his journey comes to an end.

Other Connerian Titles

The Ramblings of a Small-Town What's-His-Name, Part II

The Ramblings of a Small-Town What's-His-Name

Table 9